CHECK OUT

DEBRA PARMLEY

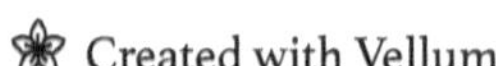 Created with Vellum

CHAPTER ONE

*S*ome people stock up on milk, bread and eggs *when a storm is coming, but book people stock up on books.*

Betsy checked out another library patron with a stack of books and wished she'd had more of a lunch break. She'd wanted to get her tire fixed. It was low, but the tire place hadn't been able to promise to have it ready in time for her to get back to work at the Bartlett Public Library in Tennessee.

Now, she'd have to drive home on that low tire in rain that had been falling all day and had now turned to sleet, which would then turn to ice as the temperature continued to drop

Wondering if it was starting to get bad out there, she pushed her glasses back up on her nose, tucked her dark blonde hair behind her right ear, a nervous habit of hers, and sent a worried look to the glass doors. She caught her breath and her mouth froze into an Oh.

Stomping into the library onto the floor mat, wearing boots and a fatigue jacket, stood a tall, broad shouldered man who took her breath away. Handsome, with long dark bangs that fell onto his face, he brushed the hair back impatiently with his right hand, fully revealing an eye patch over his right eye. His good left eye, a deep brown, bored with intensity into her. He carried a stack of books under one arm.

"Are you going to check me out or what?" The cranky elderly lady who was next in line brought Betsy back to what she should have been doing.

"Yes, ma'am." She reached for the first book with a shiver.

That man let all this cold air in, that's why I have goose bumps. Was he born in a barn? And stamping there like that with his big boots drawing attention and then giving me that look. What is that look about?

She could still feel that look. As if he'd seared it into her soul. She shivered again and finished checking out Mrs. Geraldine E. Watson. "Be safe driving home."

The woman harrumphed. "Would have been gone by now if you hadn't been googley eyeing that man. I just hope I make it home in this sleet."

I'm not googley eying anyone. Betsy frowned.

Betsy did not google eye men or flirt with them.

Her shyness prevented her from talking to men she didn't know, unless they initiated the conversation. Though she might check them out beneath lowered lids if she knew they wouldn't see her. A handsome man was a fine sight indeed.

This man, though, where had he gone? She glanced over to the door and then scanned from the door to the end of the line of patrons waiting to check out.

Oh. She took in a breath. *There he is. Right at the end of my line.*

Tension filled her. The library closing in ten minutes announcement came over the speaker, making her jump. She'd heard it so many times before, knew it was coming and yet she jumped.

Because of him. I'm jumpy because of him. It's a good thing he's not looking at me right now. I need to settle down and finish my job.

Processing the patron's books, she worked, refusing to look over at him again. But the tension did not ease.

Then he was there before her, with that dark, mysterious eye patch and strong intense deep brown eye looking at her as if he had x-ray vision and could see inside of her all the way to her soul.

They say losing one of your senses makes the others stronger. Is that why his gaze makes me feel so strange? What is he seeing? I have to say something now. He's just standing there looking at me.

This handsome stranger would have made her

feel shy even without his eye patch. The patch added a mysterious, raffish quality to his look. The frown he'd sent her way when he'd entered the library still resonated with her.

Now that intense eye was focused on her with a direct intensity she was not used to. Her words came out in a stammer. "D...did you enjoy the books?" She gave him a small, shy smile.

He met it with a growl. "Hell no, I did not enjoy these books." He pointed to his eye patch. "What do you think?"

"I...I surely don't know." She turned beet red. "I'm so sorry. I didn't think." She reached out for them. "Here, I'll just take them."

He handed them to her, still keeping that intensity focused on her.

Wanting to help him, she said, "We have audio books if these are too much."

"I'm not blind," he growled.

"Oh, of course not. I didn't mean to imply—" Flustered, she turned pink and patted the stack of books, her voice coming out in a squeak. "If the type on these is too small, we have large print." Her voice squeaked high on the word print as he impaled her with his gaze.

"My eyesight is fine," he ground out the words."

"Oh." Totally flustered now, she put one hand to her mouth, turning even redder and said, "I am so sorry. I was just trying to help."

He blinked once, his gaze changing as he seemed to catch himself, pulling back just a tad from whatever foul mood he was in, but not enough to appear friendly. "Don't worry about it." He shook his head and growled again. "Where are the audio books?"

Wordlessly, she stood pointing to the right in the direction of the audio books. She could have stepped out of Dickens' Christmas Carol as she stood so still and solemn like the ghost of Christmas future, afraid to speak, for when she spoke, it only seemed to make things worse.

He gave her a curt nod and took off in that direction.

Shakily, she let out a breath.

Less than ten minutes now and everyone will go home. I hope my tire makes it.

She carried his books to the rolling cart behind her and added them to the stack of returned books piled up.

I'll get caught up on those tomorrow. He couldn't drop the books in the return slot while the library is open because we lock it. Why people think it's funny to put their trash in that slot I'll never know. It's like unscrewing the saltshaker. Some people don't have enough interesting things to do.

Did he simply want to return the books, or had he stopped at the desk because he wanted something? He looked like he wanted something. But if so, he hadn't said what. Yet, he didn't seem like a man who had trouble speaking up. Why is he looking at me like that?

She kept checking out patrons and then with one minute to closing, there he stood before her again with two audio books in his hand. A Tom Clancy, and one of Barry Eisler's John Rain books. So, he was obviously a military man who liked action adventure stories.

You can learn a lot about a person by noting what books they check out.

He handed her the audio books without speaking, and she checked him out. His name was Nash. Nash Ware.

Ware. Be wary. He might be a werewolf.

She mentally shook herself.

Enough of the word play. I scare myself sometimes. My mind is too often in the world of fiction. He's just a man.

"Thanks." He gave a brief nod and headed for the door.

He was the last patron out and she locked the door behind him.

After shutting down lights and computer systems and putting the phone on the answering machine, she put on her coat, slipped out of her work shoes into her new black suede boots, grabbed her purse and headed for the back door.

June had left five minutes before in a hurry to pick up her baby and to get them home as soon as she could to be off the roads before the ice got worse. The library was quiet, dark and securely locked.

Walking to her car, Betsy nearly slipped on the sheets of ice that had formed. Her new boots proved to be more decorative than useful. Fortunately, she righted herself with some fancy footwork. Her car stood alone beneath the light, layered in a covering of snow and ice. Taking her glove, she brushed off the window and door of the driver's side and unlocked her door. A big black Jeep was at the parking lot entrance. It backed up, and then turned around and headed her way. The Jeep had big black tires, tinted windows and was the largest Jeep she'd ever seen.

Oh no. Who is that and what do they want? It looks like something out of the movies, like a dark government vehicle. Why are they coming toward me?

She jumped into the car quickly and locked the door, her heart racing. Putting her key in the ignition, she cranked the engine. It wouldn't start.

Oh, no.

She gasped and then turned it over again. This time it started. The stereo blasted Celtic Woman, Betsy jumped and turned it off. She couldn't see through the other windows, which she hadn't cleared off yet, so she strained to see where the Jeep had gone.

A knock on her door made her jump with a shriek and flip her head around.

The man with the intense eye and eye patch stood looking down at her.

Oh, my God. What does he want?

He held out an ice scraper and shouted through the window. "I'm going to clear your windows."

Oh. That's nice. I didn't expect that. But that doesn't mean I should trust him.

"Thank you," she shouted back, not willing to roll that window down even a crack.

He moved to the front of the car and started working on clearing it. Then he moved all the way around the car, scraping the ice off and soon all the windows were cleared. She could see out again. His Jeep was large, dark and rugged looking, parked beside her in the blind spot she hadn't cleared on the windows at first.

Just the sort of vehicle a military man or veteran would drive.

He came back to the window and looked in. Nice as he had been, she still wasn't rolling down the window.

"Thank you," she shouted again.

He nodded and touched his hat, his dark eye watching her. He walked back to his Jeep.

She watched him go wondering why he'd still been here when she locked up. If he hadn't done such a nice thing and then walked away, she would have assigned a bad motivation to the fact he was still here when she went to get into her car. She slowly backed out of the parking space.

Something is wrong.

Pulling out of reverse to drive she headed for the street, but the car slid and her rear tire hit something.

His Jeep pulled up beside her. Faster than she could work out what was wrong he was out the door and knocking at her window.

"You have a flat," he shouted.

Oh no. I should have guessed. I should've gotten it fixed at lunch, late to work or not. Now what am I going to do?

She unlocked the door, opened it and got out of the car. As she stepped onto the icy parking lot her foot slipped.

His hand shot out and grabbed her elbow before she could fall on the ice. "Careful."

"Oh." She gasped at the contact. "Thank you."

"My pleasure, ma'am."

So, he had manners after all.

They walked to the side of the car together with him holding her arm until they stopped and stood looking down at her flattened tire.

"It's not safe for you to drive," he said. "I'll give you a ride home."

Wait. What?

Flustered by all that had happened, and happened so fast, she looked up at him.

So tall.

Her capacity for words strung into a full sentence seemed to have left her.

Tall and strong.

She stared at him wide-eyed.

And close. Very close.

If she'd had to describe him in one word, she would have chosen intense. This man was intense.

"I...I'll just go back inside. I can call..." her voice trailed off.

Who could she call? None of her girlfriends were going to come out in this weather, and she had no family in town.

"Don't be afraid. You're safe with me." His calm, deep tone was reassuring, as well as his presence. "We haven't been introduced properly. I'm Nash. Nash Ware."

She came back to herself enough to speak. "Nice to meet you, Nash. I'm Betsy Bobbin. Thank you for your help."

"You're welcome, Betsy Bobbin." His tone was both a caress and a reassurance, which held a note of humor as a slow grin spread across his face when he spoke her name. The grin and the twinkle in his eye began to dash away the misgivings she had about accepting a ride from him. His was a kind eye, now that the intensity had eased, and the eye patch didn't make him appear as sinister without that intensity.

"Yes, that's me. One of three Bobbins sisters."

He continued to grin.

"I'm the oldest." Huge snowflakes were now falling and one splattered on her nose making her blink and adding spots onto her glasses.

"Well, Betsy Bobbin." Again that grin appeared as he spoke, "Let's get you home and warm and we can deal with your car later."

She hesitated. "All I know about you is your name. That's not enough to get in a car with a stranger. What do you do, Nash Ware?"

"I'm a Marine veteran. Been back about eight months. Going to college now on the G.I. bill."

"Thank you for your service."

He nodded. "You're welcome." He spoke in a quiet tone.

She stood watching him, not sure what to do. He seemed nice enough, but still, she had only his word that he was who he said he was.

"Here." He reached into his back pocket and pulled out his wallet, flipping it open to his I.D.

She looked from him to the I.D. and nodded. "Okay. I'm just going to make a phone call first."

"Whatever makes you feel more comfortable."

She took her phone out of her coat pocket and dialed June who answered on the first ring. "Hey, June. You get home okay?"

June answered that she had.

"Good. Listen, I have a flat. And I'm still at the

library. But one of our patrons, Nash Ware, was still here, and he's offered to give me a ride home."

June said he seemed like a reliable enough man, but to call her the minute she got home.

"Yes. I'll call you when I get there. Thanks, June." She hung up and then nodded at Nash. "Okay. Sorry, I just..." she shrugged.

"Do not apologize for taking precautions for your safety. Never apologize for that." He held out his hand for her again and she took it, then stepped gingerly over to the driver's side, reached in and turned the car off.

"Take anything out that might tempt a thief."

"Oh, right." She nodded with a frown. She hadn't thought of that, but who knew when she could get back to get her car if this storm continued.

She gathered her purse, closed the driver's side door and opened the back door. Taking a bag, she stuffed the pile of books into it and went to set it on the ground beside her as her purse slid off her shoulder and down her arm.

"Here, let me take that." He reached out his hand and she handed him the bag of heavy books.

His expression showed amusement. But what did he expect? She was a librarian and loved books. Her car and her house were always full of books.

From the pile of stuff in the back seat, she extracted another bad and began looking for her puppets. Puppy, kitten and bear all went into the bad. "Oh good, there's lion," she said, and then realized she was talking to herself.

"Lion?" he asked in that amused tone of voice.

She slipped lion on her hand and turned to face him, holding the bag. "Yes, lion. See? Grrrr."

He threw his head back and laughed which lit up his whole face. He was beautiful when he laughed. She'd never thought a man beautiful before.

Eye patch be damned, the man was perfect.

She gave him a huge smile in return and said, "For when I read to the children."

"Right." He nodded. "Gotcha." And that left eye gave her a slow wink.

That is the sexiest wink I have ever seen.

"Is that all of them?"

"All of? Oh. Yes. The puppets. Yes, it is."

Why can't I think straight when I'm around this man? How hard is it to string a simple sentence? I probably sound like a dimwit.

He held out his hand again.

She handed him the bag and said, "Just a few more things."

He nodded.

She turned back to the car digging for the blue dress with the white ruffled apron and the blonde curly wig that went with it all. She stood again with the items gathered into her arms.

He gave her another grin. "Halloween costume?"

"Mother Goose." Her cheeks heated. "Or Bo Peep. Depending on the occasion."

"I see."

"There's a, um, shepherds crook. In the trunk. But I can leave that."

"If you're sure now," his voice was teasing.

"I'm sure."

"Okay, hand them over and I'll load them in the back of the Jeep."

She silently handed the items to him, her cheeks still warm. Strange how warm they were with how cold it was outside, and it was terribly cold. She shivered as she realized how chilled her toes now were and looked down.

Apparently these new suede boots are not waterproof. Damn it.

"I just need one more thing." She turned back to her car and dug through papers, a couple sweaters and a sweatshirt on the floor of the car where she found her slippers.

Her pink bunny slippers.

Turning, with her cheeks blazing, her toes freezing and snow that had now turned back into sleet falling down into her face, she stood facing him, holding the slippers.

He let out a hearty laugh. "Now why am I not surprised?"

She hung her head a little sheepishly, feeling like a twelve year old.

He took them from her and opened the passenger door on his Jeep. "Get in, it's getting worse out. I'll lock your car."

She climbed in; he placed the slippers in back and then he said, "Do you have your keys?"

"Yes." She patted her coat pocket, and they jingled.

"Good." He closed her door, locked her car and then came around to the driver's side and climbed in. Closing his door and turning up the heat, he pulled toward the street. Then he turned to her and said, "Where to?"

She gave him her address, and they chatted for a bit, then he concentrated on driving through the icy sleet that was now coming down harder.

His cell phone was sitting on the charger and it buzzed as a text came in.

"Do you mind checking that for me?" He didn't look at her as he concentrated on the road conditions.

"Sure, I'm happy to," she said. She picked up the phone and looked at it.

Package is delayed.

She read the text to him.

"Send back when can I expect it?"

She typed his message in and hit send.

The phone buzzed with a response. "Two more days," she read to him.

"Tell them thanks."

She typed in the message and put the phone back.

"Thank you," he said.

"You're welcome."

She was wondering what "the package" was; it sounded so mysterious, and she didn't really know this guy, this Marine veteran with an eye patch. Already she was imagining a drug deal or something dangerous like in the movies. She squirmed in her seat.

They always talked like that, using phrases like "the package."

He glanced over at her then back to the road.

"It's a replacement frame for my Harley," he said.

"Oh. Okay," she said.

"I'm restoring a 2003 Harley Davidson Road King, one hundredth anniversary special."

"I don't know much about bikes. Why does it need a new frame? Was it wrecked?"

"Yes. I bought it wrecked. The frame was bent so I had to disassemble the whole bike and send the frame to Harley Davidson so they could destroy it before they'd send me another one."

"Why couldn't they just send you a new one?"

"Number of the frame has to match the number on the engine and the title. Lots of bikes get stolen. It's a good thing really, but it's also a pain in the ass."

"Yes, I can see that it would be." She nodded. "Were you a mechanic in the Marines?"

"No. Though I can work on some things." He shrugged.

He might not think disassembling and reassembling a motorcycle was a big deal, but she sure did.

There was something sexy and primal about a man who was capable and could fix things.

"How did the bike get wrecked?"

"No idea. I bought it before my last tour. Just never had time to work on it until a few months ago. I wasn't home much."

"I see," she said.

He drove in silence.

Betsy sat thinking of how she'd never gotten to know any Marines or guys that drove Harleys. Until now when this handsome, growly guy had walked into her library and her life with his mood. Strong, sure and more than slightly dangerous, she wondered what had made him so moody. He'd tempered himself getting control of that mood so that he was more than pleasant to be around now, but she wondered why he'd been so growly when he first spoke to her.

She was more than a little bit curious and wanted to know more about him, but he was concentrating on the road, so she remained silent. Though her imagination was taking her to all sorts of places. Right on the back of his bike.

Nash Ware stepped into the library wearing another frown and fighting another damned headache as he stomped his feet to knock the slush off his boots.

Then he saw her.

A pretty little, dark blonde with curves, wearing red-rimmed glasses which framed pretty green eyes and red lipstick upon lips formed into an oh.

Not the sort of librarian he'd expected to see behind the counter. Standing there staring at him with that pouty little oh on her face. He'd like to kiss those pouty lips.

But she was like all the other women who liked to stare at his eye patch. He was never going to get used to that. He was also probably never going to get laid again. Course there wasn't much point in trying when he kept having these damned headaches.

He'd given up on trying to finish reading any of the books he'd checked out. Reading seemed to bring them on, or maybe it was the dreams he'd been having, but whatever it was, since he wasn't enjoying reading the books, he was bringing them back to the library. He'd planned to ask if they had any of the books on his reading list, which might save him some money in the college bookstore.

The pouty little miss had turned back to the other patrons and was checking them out and pointedly ignoring him after staring.

He got in line and waited his turn while

watching her in a covert way, hoping she wouldn't notice.

Googely eyes, huh. The old woman had to be wrong. Pouty miss didn't like that much. If I didn't have this headache I'd be tempted to kiss her.

She was the most adorable little librarian he had ever seen.

But she was afraid of the eye patch and him. A fresh wave of pain coursed through his head.

By the time he stood before her, he was in between waves of pain. He knew he'd snapped at her and on another day he might have apologized. But he didn't. Instead, he went to the audio section with her reactions running through his mind.

I'm not fucking blind. Damn it.

Her reaction had angered him more than he was comfortable with. But he hated the way women looked at him now, either in fear or with pity or curiosity. And to add her to the list of women who had reacted that way, well, it was too damn much.

He'd calmed down by the time she checked him out and when he walked to his car he popped in an audio tape, thinking he'd start listening to it on the way home. If he couldn't read the fiction he enjoyed so much, he could listen on the way to appointments or to class. He'd save his eye for reading the course work and stick to that.

The story had just started to play and he would have driven off, but then he noticed that the other librarian had pulled out of the parking lot and headed for home, and there was only one other car in the lot with his.

It had to belong to the pouty little librarian.

I'll just wait and see that she gets her car started before I go. Where the hell is their security? She shouldn't be walking to her car at night alone, even in good weather.

CHAPTER TWO

"You don't have a security guard."

He'd said it like a statement, but she knew he was really asking a question. "Small libraries like ours don't have the budget for it."

"You shouldn't be walking to your car at night alone. It's too isolated."

"Sometimes we have a police car swing by, so they do patrol."

"Not tonight."

"No, not tonight. I'm glad you were here."

"Me too. Do you need to pick up anything at the store before I drop you off?"

"No. Even if I get snowed in tomorrow, I have everything I need."

Except a car that is safe to drive.

They rode in silence and she wondered about his radio.

Maybe it didn't work.

He had a CD player, but she didn't see any CD's other than the ones he'd gotten at the library.

Maybe he wasn't a music person.

"What kind of music do you like?"

"Hard rock, heavy metal."

She didn't know much about heavy metal and had hoped he'd name a band or two so they'd have something to talk about.

The silence seemed to stretch and then he said, "Have you worked at the library long?"

"Three years. I moved here from Ohio."

"So you're used to snow?"

"Yes, but people here don't know how to drive in it." Wanting to keep the conversation going she asked, "Where are you from?"

"Born in Texas, spent half my childhood in Mississippi."

"You don't have much of an accent. From either place."

"I've lived a lot of places."

"I'll bet you have a lot of interesting stories to tell."

He simply grunted and then went silent again.

This time she didn't push against the silence. She wished she hadn't made that comment.

His phone buzzed, and he asked her to read the

message to him and to relay answers. That was good because she wasn't all that comfortable with the silences. She didn't know him well enough to be. She was glad when the messages came in, and she could do something to help as well as it giving them something to talk about.

So he had a Harley. Her imagination was now doing all sorts of wild things with that information. And then they were at her home pulling in.

Nash pulled into her driveway, eyed the darkened house as he put the Jeep in park and then turned to her. "Do you live alone?"

"Yes. Just me and my books." She smiled. That was the line she always told her sister. She'd had a live in boyfriend once, but that had been a huge mistake. She couldn't get a minute to herself to read when he was home. It was like he took it as a personal affront the moment she stuck her nose in a book.

Nash nodded, got out and came around to open her door. Holding his hand out, he waited for her to take hold and climb down. "I'll check the house, get you inside and then I'll carry your things in."

Placing her hand in his, she said, "Thank you."

The icy snow beneath her feet was slippery and her damp boots were the most impractical winter shoes she had ever bought. She'd have been better off wearing her tennis shoes. Even if they got wet, they'd have had some traction at least.

Wait. Check the house. He'll what? That was an odd phrase.

She looked up at him as they walked toward the front door together. He held her hand in case she fell. "What did you mean check the house?"

"Just to make sure it's safe."

She frowned. "Why wouldn't it be safe?"

He took a deep breath. "Just indulge me, okay? I want to know you are safe."

"Well, okay." It seemed silly to her, this was Bartlett after all, not Memphis where the crime rate was high. But on the other hand, it was rather sweet, and Memphis was just a few streets over. She just wasn't used to anyone looking out for her safety since she'd moved here. None of her family lived in Tennessee, and she'd only been here three years.

At the door, she fished her keys out of her purse and then placed it in the lock.

"Let me go in first," he said.

"All right." She unlocked the door and then stepped back as he pushed the door open and entered.

He radiated a powerful strength as he entered her house and moved through the rooms with her just a few steps behind him. Then he stopped and turned around to face her. "All clear."

She noted how tension visibly left his body. "Good." She smiled. "Thank you for checking."

"Any time." He nodded. "I'll get your things.

Maybe you ought to call your friend now so she won't worry."

"Oh, yes." She'd completely forgotten about June. "I'll do that." She dialed her cell phone as he went out the front door.

June answered right away. "You okay? I thought you'd be home before now."

"Yes, I'm fine. Nash is just bringing my things in."

"Nash is still there." Betsy could hear June smile through the phone. "You should offer him some coffee."

"No, he will be going soon."

"What a pity. That man is built. I'd love to see him with his shirt off."

"June, it's a little cold for that."

"You could warm him up. Stoke his fire. Be his burning ember."

"Go back to whatever romance novel you were reading." Betsy laughed.

"Think of it, Betsy. Him without his shirt."

"June, I've got to go now."

Nash had just entered holding her things.

She looked up at him, images of how he might look without his shirt now filling her head. He filled out his jeans well too, those muscular thighs evident.

June was saying goodbye, but Betsy barely heard as she clicked off the phone, her mouth suddenly dry.

Nash looked at her, as she slowly turned red.

He'd caught her glancing from his shoulders down to his boots. She was definitely googly eying him now. She could not get those images out of her mind, and he'd caught her looking.

Betsy stood completely tongue tied as her face heated. She tucked her hair behind her right ear and looked down.

"Where shall I put these?"

"Oh." Her voice squeaked as she looked at him again. "Just anywhere."

Oh no. It's the incomplete sentences again.

He set the things on an armchair near the door. "Okay." He pulled a piece of paper and a pen out of his pocket and wrote his number down. "In case you need me, this is my number. I'm only ten minutes away."

"Oh. Good. Thank you."

"Would you be comfortable giving me your number?"

"Oh, yes." She rattled it off for him, and he put it into his cell phone.

"Thanks." He stowed his phone away in his pocket. "All right. Get a good night's sleep. I'll check on you tomorrow, and we'll see about that tire."

"Oh." He was heading for the door and she hurried over to him. "Yes, you too. Safe travels."

He opened the door, stepped out and stood facing her. "Lock up tight."

"Yes, I will."

"Oh and hey. About snapping at you today. I want to apologize."

"It's okay."

"No, it's not. I had a bad headache and I was taking my bad mood out on you."

"Oh. Well, apology accepted. Is your headache gone?"

"It's manageable."

"Well, I hope you feel better soon."

"Thanks. Good night, Betsy."

"Good night, Nash." She closed the door and locked the lock and the deadbolt. Then she let out a sigh. It had been quite an exciting night at the library. She smiled.

He really is nice once you get to know him a little bit. Well, more than nice. He is hot.

THE NEXT MORNING her phone rang around ten. "Hello?"

"Betsy, this is Nash."

"Oh, good morning."

"Morning. Did you sleep well?"

"Yes. Like a baby."

"Good. About the tire. I have a spare I can put on and then drive it wherever you were planning to have tires put on."

"Oh, it's already at Gateway Tire. I called the

AAA road service and had it towed there. They're putting tires on it this afternoon, and said they'd call when it's ready."

"I see. Do you need a ride to go pick it up once it's done?"

"No. I'm good. But thanks for offering."

Her independent streak was doing a women can roar snow dance on the front lawn as she looked out the front window and talked to him. She'd had AAA tow the car, and she would take a taxi to pick it up. This was how she'd operated since she came to the Memphis area. Bartlett was a nice community town, but she just didn't know anyone she could impose on the way she'd have to in order to take care of her car. She really could take care of herself.

He was silent for a minute and then he said, "Would you like to have dinner with me next Friday?"

"No, I can't. My little sister is in town for a visit that weekend."

"Okay. Well, enjoy your visit."

"Yes. We will. And thank you again for your help last night."

"You're welcome."

She didn't know what to say next, and the silence was making her nervous. "Okay, I have to run now. See you at the library."

"See you there. Bye."

"Bye."

He hung up the phone, and she sat staring at it.

Shit. He asked me for a date. I can't believe it. Wait til June hears. It's too bad I can't go. He might not ask me out again. Did I say it right?

She had a sinking feeling she had come off sounding like she wasn't interested and was using her sister's visit as an excuse for something she didn't want to do anyway.

But it wasn't like that at all.

I hope he asks me out again.

A WEEK LATER, her sister Leann arrived, and Betsy forgot about Nash Ware. The weather had cleared; ice and snow melting, and it had even begun to warm up just in time for her sister's visit. Between working at the library and running around town with her little sister, there was scarcely time to think of anything else.

Leann, a junior in college, was taking a semester off from classes, but apparently not from partying.

Betsy had never seen her sister so animated. It was her first visit to Memphis, and she wanted to see and do everything from Graceland, to the M bridge and the pyramid, to Beale Street. Betsy had been running Leann all over town.

Today was Friday and Betsy was working at the library. Her sister had borrowed the car and gone shopping. She came in right around lunchtime, and brought Betsy a sandwich. "Hey sis, you'll never guess what I bought us."

"I dare say you're right. What did you get us?"

"Ooh, I can't tell you yet. It's a surprise."

"Okay then, I will be surprised."

"We can wear them when we go out tonight."

"Oh, we can?"

The front door opened and Nash Ware walked in.

Both sisters turned to watch him, Leann following Betsy's gaze.

"Ooh, now he is hot in that pirate, mercenary, stud kind of way. Rawr."

"He is, isn't he?"

Nash came up to the desk and handed in his books.

Betsy took them with a smile. "Thank you."

"Welcome."

"Nash, I'd like you to meet my sister, Leann. She's on break from Eastern Kentucky and is here visiting."

"Nice to meet you."

"Nice to meet you too." Leann practically purred, and for the first time in years, Betsy felt a stir of jealousy toward her sister. Younger and with no problems talking to or flirting with men, Leann had always had a string of boyfriends.

"Anything else I can do for you, Nash?" Betsy

knew her tone sounded dismissive, but she just wanted him away from her sister before something horrible happened like him asking Leann out.

"No. I'm good." Nash nodded and then moved away toward the bookracks.

"I'll just bet he is," Lean muttered under her breath.

"So where are we going tonight?" Betsy hoped changing the subject would redirect Leann away from Nash.

A huge grin filled LeAnn's face and she said, "The Electric Cowboy."

"Oh, country western. That sounds fun. I always wanted to learn to line dance." Betsy nodded.

Nash, who was just around the corner looking at books he had no interest in, overheard them and smiled.

Perfect.

He was meeting his buds for a beer and that was as good a place as any to do it. Maybe he could get Betsy to dance with him. The Texas two-step was one dance he knew well.

THE ELECTRIC COWBOY WAS CROWDED, but Nash could have picked out Betsy in any crowd. Her long dark blonde hair, heart shaped face and that pouty mouth wearing red lipstick drew him like a magnet.

Her sister stood out too, though in a louder bleach blonde way. She was a party girl, no doubt. The three empty margarita glasses lined up in front of Leann compared to the one in front of Betsy pointed out the differences in the two sisters.

Nash preferred the understated beauty of the librarian. He could get lost in her eyes and spend hours kissing that red mouth. Tonight Betsy was wearing blue jeans, low boots and a white eyelet, sleeveless blouse with a red ribbon run through the neckline, which only enhanced the red lipstick she wore. The all American girl next-door look fit her perfectly. The impression she gave when he looked at her was a sweet young woman with a slightly naughty side, if the lipstick was an indicator.

If she wasn't naughty, she wanted to be.

He'd bet money on that.

Leann on the other hand, was wearing a tight, black, leather skirt she looked like she'd been poured into, high, black boots and a red t-shirt that said dangerous spelled out in silver across her chest. She was wearing a black, straw cowgirl hat atop her long blonde hair.

Betsy was wearing a white one, which contrasted with her pretty dark blonde hair.

The girls had been dancing, mostly line dances as that was all that was being played until just now. They'd taken the *learn a new line dance lesson* and then danced a few others. Nash had watched them in between hanging out with his Marine buddies, Pete, Lance and Jim.

"Which one?" Jim leaned near and nudged Nash's arm.

Nash turned to look at Jim, wondering what he'd missed. Betsy's kissable lips were such a distraction.

"Which one are you going to ask to dance? Because I'll ask the other one. They're both hotties."

"Betsy." Her name was out before he caught himself.

Jim grinned, mirth in his Irish eyes.

"Oho. So, you know these girls." Lance laughed. "Which one have you slept with?"

"Neither." This conversation was beginning to get on his nerves even though the guys were only being the guys.

"Which one is Betsy?" Pete asked.

"In the white hat, white blouse."

"Pretty little thing. The kind who will want a ring on her finger," Pete said.

"And the other one?" Jim asked.

"Leann. Her sister."

"Right," Jim stood and downed his beer. "Let's go."

James Garnet, never one to wait to go after what he wanted, would lead the way. Likely he'd charm the girls with his quick wit.

As long as he doesn't turn the charm on too much with Betsy, it's cool.

"Betsy works at the library," Nash said.

"Where you've been getting those audio books."

"Yep."

Jim got the picture and nodded.

They'd started moving toward the girls.

But the girls were on the opposite side of the bar and they were already too late. Two other guys had asked the girls to dance; they'd said yes and were headed to the dance floor.

"Well, hell." Jim turned and moved back to their table. He sat back down and signaled the waitress for another round of beers. "The next one's on me."

Nash watched as the girls danced with the other two guys. He was kicking himself for not reaching Betsy sooner and asking her onto the dance floor first.

The girls finished dancing and the two men followed them over to the bar and were hanging out. The one who'd danced with Leann ordered two shots, and they were placed in front of them. He and Leann knocked them back, and the man laughed.

Betsy did not look happy. Nash watched her have an animated conversation with her sister.

Leann and the other man headed back to the dance floor, and Betsy went toward the ladies room.

Why didn't Leann go with her? Women usually go in pairs.

Once Betsy was out of sight, Leann's dance partner started putting his hands where they didn't belong, right on her ass and sliding toward the bottom of that short, short skirt and then underneath.

Leann was laughing and letting him pull her close enough to rub against her. *She was a wild thing, but they needed to be doing that off the dance floor.*

Nash wondered what Betsy would think of her sister's behavior.

He didn't have to wait long. The moment Betsy emerged and saw her sister, her jaw dropped in shock, and then she was hurrying toward Leann.

Nash stood and started to make his way toward them. Just in case he was needed. Grown men who danced with little college girls that let them take liberties like that generally didn't take well to no's from drunken college girls or from well-meaning sisters. He'd spent enough time in bars to read the signs of a bad situation brewing.

Making his way through the crowd with Jim behind him, he saw Betsy pulling at her sister's arm trying to break the two up.

The guy wasn't having it, but another man nearby said something to him, and he let the girl go.

Betsy had her by the arm and was hurrying her to the door.

Great. They're leaving and I haven't talked to her yet. This evening is not going like I had hoped.

The dude who'd been pawing Leann had left the dance floor and was now heading outside too.

Oh, hell no.

Moving faster, Nash pushed through the crowd. He didn't like those girls being where he could not see them. He pushed through the door with Jim right behind him. Lance and Pete wouldn't be far behind once they paid for their drinks.

Outside, Leann was leaning over throwing up.

Betsy stood holding Leann's hair back, not noticing Mr. Get His Ass Kicked Soon moving toward them.

"What did you run out on me for?" Mr. G.H.A.K.S. growled. He gave Betsy a rough push; her back hit the side of the building, and pulled Leann to him. "This filly is mine."

"No! Get your filthy hands off my sister." Betsy screamed as she came toward him again and grabbed his arm, trying to pull him away. "She's drunk. She doesn't know what she's doing. Let her go!"

"Stay back, bitch," he snarled, shaking her off his arm as if she were nothing. "She promised me a good time, and you ain't getting in the way."

Betsy didn't know what to do, as she tried to pull him away from Leann.

Oh my God, he's got my sister. He's going to take her.

"Let go of her!" Betsy's scream was frantic and full of fear. She didn't know how to stop him. He was too strong, and he had her baby sister who she'd protected and looked after all her life.

"You heard the lady." Nash's tone behind her allowed for no argument and was as much a command as a warning.

She turned her head, saw him and her breath caught.

Nash. Where had he come from?

The man looked over at Nash in surprise and then seeing him approaching, sneered as he pulled Leann closer. "You ain't gonna stop me, one eye."

Click.

Nash moved fast, the knife opening in one hand, a fluid motion as he stepped closer grabbing the man's shirt with his other hand. "Think again."

Then with another swift move, Nash spun the man around away from Leann.

Betsy let loose a breath. Leann was free. But not out of danger as the drunken man lurched toward Leann again, missing her this time as Betsy pulled her back away from his reach.

"Damn you." The man roared, "Fucking jarhead." As he came toward Nash with his fists up.

Three tough looking military men now stood behind Nash, to provide backup, but they stood with their arms crossed watching as if confident they weren't needed. And maybe they weren't.

Nash was a Marine, trained to fight. The look in his eyes said he could kill. With one swift move, he closed the knife and put it back in his pocket. Raising his arms as the man charged, he watched, hands angled, as he stood intent and ready to strike.

He'd put away the knife? Why did Nash put away the knife? Wouldn't the knife be better than using his hands? And why didn't the other man run instead of picking a fight with a Marine?

Betsy had never seen men fight in person, only on TV and in movies. The fierce swiftness with which Nash stopped the man from taking Leann left her blinking, still trying to grapple with what had just happened. And now he was looking at the man as if he wanted this fight. As if he'd take pleasure in beating the man to a pulp.

The drunken man was no match for him and was stupidly convinced he was invincible.

The man lunged and missed. Couldn't get a punch in as Nash moved faster with one swift side chop of his hand to the man's neck. The man dropped onto the cement, then Nash was down on the ground with him ready to hit him again.

One of his buddies stepped forward and stopped him. "That's enough, bro," he said, "back off.'

Nash stopped then and seemed to clear his head, the rage moving away from him.

Betsy had moved to put her arms around her sister, and he looked up at them, seeing they were both safe, then he tore his fierce gaze away and nodded at his buddy.

Nash was one bad ass. She was glad he'd

protected them, but this other side of him she was seeing scared her. She'd never been around any kind of violence.

Fighting was something men did in movies, or overseas to defend our country, not something they did in front of her in parking lots on a Friday night.

Going to bars on the weekend really wasn't her thing. She liked watching movies or staying home and reading a good book. She'd read stories with fights in them but nothing she had seen or read compared with what had just happened. The fierce side of Nash scared her.

Would he have stopped if his buddy hadn't stopped him? Is he the kind of violent man who might turn on me one day?

All was still and the only thing Betsy heard was Leann softly sobbing. Then her sister spoke. "I'm sorry, Bets. I'm sorry, I'm sorry."

Betsy gathered her closer in a hug and stroked her hair. "It's okay, hun. You're okay. I'm going to get you home and get you cleaned up."

But she just kept repeating the word sorry as if she hadn't heard.

Nash turned to gaze at her and he took them both in. He cleared his throat. "You both okay?"

Betsy nodded.

"He didn't hurt you?"

She shook her head no. "You stopped him in time," she nearly whispered, her voice quiet in the silent parking lot. Inside, country tunes played and were momentarily louder as people exited the bar. None of the other patrons had witnessed the fight.

He nodded. "Good."

"Oh my God," a woman said, "What happened?"

"Just another drunk," Nash's redheaded friend said. "I'll go in and tell them to call for a taxi. Take care of things here." He nodded to Nash and headed inside.

"Take her home, Betsy," Nash said. "I'll follow you, make sure you get in okay."

"No." She held out a hand toward him as if to warn him off. "I don't want you following me. We're fine."

She didn't want him coming to her house and following. She didn't want him in her house when she was afraid of him.

His three buddies stood looking at her.

They had to be military or ex-military. It was in their build and their bearing. They were the defenders. The good guys. She knew this, but something about Nash still scared her.

Betsy tried to shake away the feelings she now had toward Nash and to remember to be grateful. Because she was. God only knows what that man would have done to either of them, and now her baby sister was safe.

"Thank you, Nash." She paused. "I will..." She frowned and looked at her sister who was still muttering her litany of sorry. Then she looked back at him and then down. "Thank you for stopping him. I've got to get her home. I will...call you...later...and let you know how she is."

He watched her wordlessly, taking everything in. Her gratitude, her hesitation, that fear in her eyes like the first night they'd met when he'd knocked on her window. He'd thought the fear banished. Dammit, now it was back.

"Be safe going home." He couldn't keep the sad note out of his voice. God, he'd only wanted to keep her safe, to keep both of them safe. But he obviously still had some work to do to get over this anger he was carrying inside.

This guy had not been that big of a threat. Nash normally would have taken care of the problem easily without losing his cool. But he had and if his buddy hadn't called him off there's no telling what he'd have done. He'd likely be in jail now.

Nash hated that she'd seen how angry he'd become. Hated to see fear in her eyes. He'd never hurt her. Hell, he'd cut off his right arm before he'd hurt her. But she didn't know that. She hardly knew him at all. And what she did know, she was now afraid of.

It was one of the saddest nights of his life as he watched her go.

CHAPTER THREE

*B*etsy's cell phone cheeped after they'd been home about two minutes. It was Nash.

Just want to know you made it home safe.

She texted him back. *Yes, home safe, thank you.*

She didn't tell him she'd had to pull over twice for her sister to be sick out the side of the car, and that she didn't even have her in the house yet and still had to clean up her car.

You're welcome. I have to go.

Night.

Night. Thank you.

Any time, darlin'.

Betsy put her phone away and went to help Leann into the house.

Leanne had said, "I'm sorry" so many times Betsy couldn't stand it anymore. The moment Betsy got her in through the front door she lost it. "Sorry is a sorry word," she snapped. "Stop it, Leann."

That just sent her sister into a rush of tears as her words rushed out. "Didn't mean to cause trouble. Be a burden. Get your boyfriend in trouble."

"Oh, for heaven's sake." Betsy helped her over to the couch and made her sit. "He's not in trouble."

"But the police."

"There were no police." She walked over to the door to lock and deadbolt it.

"Police always come." Leann sobbed. "Bar fights. Always."

"Geesh Leann. What all have you been getting into in Kentucky?"

"No trouble, I swear."

"Uh huh." Betsy didn't believe her. In fact her little sister had changed so much. She was alarmed at the rate Leann could knock back a margarita.

Tequila had never been an easy thing for Betsy to drink, but Leann had knocked back three of them pretty fast, and then started doing shots.

She's obviously been doing some partying at Eastern Kentucky University. Is she taking a semester off because her grades have fallen? What is really going on?

"You don't b'lieve me." Off Leann went with another round of sobbing.

"Leann," Betsy said with a sigh. "We'll talk about all this in the morning. Now, let's get you into bed so you can sleep it off."

"'Kay." Leann sniffled.

Leann allowed Betsy to lead her into the bedroom and help her into bed. Betsy took one look at the tight leather skirt and shook her head.

She'll just have to sleep like that. I'm not even going to attempt to wrestle her out of that thing. If she's uncomfortable, it's her own fault and serves her right. Maybe she won't do this again.

She pulled a blanket up over her sister and gave a sigh.

It's a good thing our parents aren't alive to see how their youngest is behaving.

Betsy paused by the doorway before she turned out the light and let her anger fade. It had been hard on all of them after losing their dad four years ago. She'd thought everything was going fine.

Leann was in college planning to go into marketing, and Virginia had a thriving wedding photography business she ran out of the old family home.

Maybe I'd better call Virginia in the morning and see if she knows anything. Leann might have confided in her.

Betsy closed the door with a sigh. With her sister safely asleep for the night, her thoughts returned to Nash. He'd been wonderful, coming to the rescue twice now. Definitely a man of action, hero type. The way he looked out for her would have made her feel safe and secure around him, except for the look she'd seen on his face.

He could have killed the other man easily. Yet, he hadn't.

It reminded her of her first impression and the fact she didn't really know him. He'd asked her out once and she'd hoped he would ask again. He was intimidating and she'd been afraid of him at first.

If he hadn't been at the bar tonight ... Leann might have been... well, she didn't want to think about that

She wanted to get ready for bed as she realized she was exhausted. *It had been a long night.* But there was still her car to be cleaned up. She had to take care of cleaning it before she could go to bed. There was no chance of leaving it and insisting her sister clean it up tomorrow. Betsy had to be at work bright and early to open the library. She'd have to confront her sister about the evening events after work tomorrow.

NASH READ Betsy's text message and felt a sense of relief. The ladies were home safe. He'd been tempted to follow Betsy home just to make sure of that, but she might have misconstrued it, and he wanted no more misunderstandings between them.

Her car was running fine, the tire was fixed, and the guy who wouldn't take no for an answer had been dealt with. All was righted again, and he wanted it to stay that way.

This was the second time she'd needed rescuing. He'd much rather have been taking her on a dinner date or to the movies so they could get to know each other without some damn crisis or another going on. He was not a fan of females who were constantly in crisis.

He'd had enough of that with his ex-fiancé, Nicole, and all her little dramas. While he'd been dodging RPG's, she was whining about herself and what she was going through. Those little dramas, which she brought upon herself, were incongruent when he'd just lost one of his buddies and had to write a letter home to his buddy's wife. After that phone call home to Nicole, he'd been ready to call it quits as soon as he was stateside again and could do it in person. So, her breaking it off had not come as a shock or a surprise. It was what needed to happen.

The look of revulsion in her eyes when she saw him with the eye patch made him wish they'd broken up over the phone.

If he hadn't insisted they meet in person to talk, hadn't persisted in doing things the right way, he'd never have seen her expression.

Nicole wanted everything to be beautiful and perfect. Appearances were important to her. She was fashion model beautiful and enchanting until he got to know her other side, which she hid well.

Tonight her words rang through his head again,

along with the image of her expression as that pretty lip of hers curled up in an ugly way.

I can't be married to a man with one eye. I don't want my children looking at that from their crib when they wake up.

Babies. He hadn't even considered babies or what his future children might think. Her words had driven deep. Nicole couldn't just say she was done and that they were through. She had to inflict damage as she left, not caring that she'd hurt him.

Betsy was completely different than Nicole. She didn't seem the type to seek drama or to create her own crisis, making everything about her. Thoughts of Betsy and what he did know of her made him smile.

A shy librarian who looked out for her little sister. Not into fashions or partying. Not much of a drinker. Likes to wear red lipstick. Reads to children.

This was the sweet woman he wanted to date and get to know better.

Both times she'd needed rescuing were events she couldn't have prevented.

Hopefully, there wouldn't be any more events. Though he was happy to step in if she needed him.

What he wanted most was a quiet life, having had enough of drama and war.

But I can't ask her out again. Not when she looks at me with fear in her eyes. Fear or revulsion.

If that is how women feel when they look at me,

might as well give up on dating. Better to be alone.

~

BETSY STOOD behind the counter at the library wondering how her sister was fairing. The hangover had left her moaning for Betsy to leave her alone in the morning, so Betsy hadn't attempted to talk to her before heading to work, beyond saying she was leaving for work now.

Virginia's phone had gone to voice mail, saying she was on a photo shoot and would return calls later. There'd been no chance to discuss their baby sister.

Replaying the events of last night in her head, she wondered how Nash had been there, so quick, to intervene at the bar before something bad could happen.

He must have been there with his Marine buddies heading into the bar. I am glad he happened to be there at the right time. We were lucky Nash stopped by.

The day dragged. She was still tired from the night before. A physical as well as an emotional tiredness hovered. She'd have to have a good long talk with Leann tonight. If her sister continued this way, she would end up in trouble of some kind, and Betsy didn't want that to happen.

Worry and being tired had made her cranky.

Mrs. Verte, an older lady patron with bright red

hair who covered it with black hair dye and usually had her roots showing approached the counter.

The first time Betsy had seen Mrs. Verte she had done the double take. The college girls were getting the tips of their hair colored purple or blue or red, but this was like a reverse of that and on Mrs. Verte it took some getting used to. Well, Mrs. Verte herself took some getting used to.

Oh great, here she comes again.

Betsy had already spoken to Mrs. Verte once on the phone this morning about the books she was looking for, so she could have guessed what the answer was, but she had to ask just the same.

Placing a smile on her face, Betsy said, "Hello, Mrs. Verte. What can I help you with today?"

"I need books on those lizards. Any kind of lizard in Florida. I leave on a trip to visit my girlfriend from high school, Susan Weston, in three weeks. Time is running out. I haven't seen her since high school. She's moved back from Europe now that her husband died. Terrible thing losing a husband. And to be over there by herself? Well, I cannot imagine. This is my first trip to Florida."

Oh no. She's going to go on and on again. Before we ever get to the books.

Like a poorly written novel, Mrs. Verte would pour out her entire back-story of why she was checking out a book instead of simply asking for it. Instead of asking for a book on lizards native to Florida, which would have been the simplest thing to do, or instead of asking for a book on lizards, which would tell if any of them were poisonous, again simpler than her long rambling way, here she went again.

"Books on lizards? Let me pull that information for you." Betsy hoped to redirect the woman's course back to the books she wanted.

"Now, Susan, she never was good at science, so she won't know about those lizards. She swears none of them are poisonous, but she hasn't lived there long enough to know. And she needs to know!" Mrs. Verte's voice rose as she expressed alarm for her friend.

"Shhh. We must keep our voices down." Betsy found including herself with this admonition helped it to go over a bit smoother.

"I know, dear," Mrs. Verte leaned forward as if to whisper, though her voice never dropped that low and was likely more for dramatic affect. "Everyone doesn't need to know our business."

Had Betsy been in a better mood and less tired, she would have had to stifle her laugh as several library patrons looked their way.

Everyone always knew Mrs. Verte's business because Mrs. Verte would tell them.

But today Betsy really just wanted to say; I don't care why you are checking out these books. You've already told me once before on the phone. Please just take your books and go. I'm tired and ready to go home.

But you couldn't say that to a patron. Oh, no. You would lose your job. So instead there was nothing to do but nod, show an interest you weren't feeling at the moment to appease the woman, and pray she finished her long tale soon.

This didn't hit her all the time, but damn if Mrs. Verte didn't have a knack for appearing on the worst possible day.

"You do know we have small lizards here in Bartlett too?" Betsy said.

"I know, but they have those gators and crocodiles and lizards down there, in Florida that eat pets and small children. And the poisonous ones!"

"Well, read up on them, then you will know."

Betsy didn't have anything else to say. Mrs. Verte was so full of fears and phobias there really wasn't anything you could do for her. Except find her the books that would give her facts, which usually disproved her fears, the opposite of what she was looking for, which was confirmation she was right about them. Sometimes she wouldn't believe the facts even if they were written in a book. Probably because she didn't want to.

Tired from the night before, worried about her sister and with her thoughts returning again and again to Nash, Mrs. Verte was doubly hard to take today.

Finally, Mrs. Verte took her books and left. Betsy sighed.

Her thoughts returned to Nash.

Then, just as if she had conjured him, Nash strode through the door.

His gaze was on her as he approached the desk. Her mouth went dry, and she swallowed.

Nash had presence and that intense gaze of his was focused directly at her.

He stood before her and she had to resist the urge to wipe her palms down her skirt. Instead, she picked up a pencil and gripped it as if she would write with it.

"Hello, Betsy." His voice, deep and low, sent awareness through her body and his gaze made her feel warm as heat spread to her cheeks. "Thought I'd swing in on my way home from class and see how you were doing."

"I'm doing okay."

"And your sister?"

"Leann is dealing with the hangover and hopefully has learned her lesson."

"You're worried."

"She was sucking down that tequila pretty fast last night. So, yes, I am."

"Understandably."

"Thank you for stopping him."

"Not necessary to thank me. I was happy to do it."

"If you hadn't come along..." She shivered.

"But I did."

She smiled. "Yes, you did."

He nodded. "Just wanted to check on you."

"Thank you for caring."

"I also wanted to thank you for the audio book suggestion." He pulled one out of his pocket and handed it to her to return it. "I've been enjoying them."

"Oh, good. I'm glad."

"What do you like to read?"

"Me? I read a little bit of everything."

"What's your favorite genre?"

Simone passed behind Betsy and overhearing the conversation said, "Betsy likes romance. Goes through about three of those a week. She likes the hearts and flowers and happy ever afters."

"So, romance." Nash grinned.

"Yes, I like reading romance." Betsy wondered where this was going.

"Well, my next question was going to be who is your favorite author? But I won't have read them if it's romance."

"I don't really have one favorite. I have many favorites."

"How's the Harley coming along? Did your frame come in?"

"It's coming along fine, and yes it did."

More patrons were lining up behind Nash and

he glanced at them, then back at her with a smile. "See you later, Betsy."

"Okay, see you later." She smiled. Seeing him really had brightened up her day.

∼

NASH WALKED from the library to his Jeep, his thoughts on the pretty librarian.

So she's hearts and flowers? That's easy enough. I just need to woo her. Slowly. One flower at a time. And time is what I have plenty of.

If he could just have the time for her to get to know him slowly, for her to learn to trust him, they might have a chance. *It was worth a try.*

Betsy was like a prize-winning flower herself. Women like her didn't come along every day.

After his appointment this morning with the pysch doctor, he was more confident about their chances. Yes, he was trained to kill, but at heart he was not a man who enjoyed killing. Taking out threats, yes. Taking down enemies, yes. That was the job he'd been trained to do. But now that he was back in the states, back in civilian life, he hoped he'd never have to use those skills.

The doctor had reminded him that he'd only been back eight months, and though he still had to work through some things, he'd progressed faster than the doctor had expected him to.

Nash was more encouraged than he'd ever been since he returned stateside. He finally had his old confidence back.

Jim's call had helped too. He'd agreed with the therapist's assessment that Betsy was initially afraid of the attacker and that fear had still had her in its grip even after Nash had stopped the attack. Things might be very different between them today. So Nash had hoped as he entered the library that Betsy was over her fear and back to normal.

Seeing Betsy had borne that out. She even seemed happy to see him again and had asked about his bike. So she was interested in that. He'd have to invite her for a ride once the bike was road worthy and tested.

He could win her with enough time and persistence. He had learned to be a patient man, to watch and to wait as the impatience of his youth had been burned away in active duty. When to be patient and when to act fast were keys to surviving and both were well honed in him. He would be patient as long as it took, and he would slowly sweep her off her feet.

So hearts and flowers it is. Wonder what her favorite flower is?

How could he find that out? Too bad her sister wasn't local so he could bump into her and ask. He'd have to try another way.

Nicole hadn't wanted the hearts and flowers,

unless they were expensive. If it didn't have a high price tag, she'd show no interest in it. It had been red roses or nothing with her.

Would Betsy like the little things? Like say a simple bouquet of wildflowers or a single bloom? Was she meant to be the girl of his heart?

He had a feeling she was, and there was only one way to find out. He would plan a campaign to woo her. One flower at a time. One patient moment at a time.

It was snowing again as he drove from the library to the grocery store and sleeting when he came out. Stowing his groceries in the Jeep, he then paused before heading back into the store. He knew just what to do.

He picked out a small card and a single pink rose bud. The card's message said, *To a sweet girl,* on the outside and once opened, the card said, *who lights up the room.* After making his second purchase, he headed back to his Jeep, climbed in and drove back to the library.

Her little car was parked beneath one of the lights in the parking lot, which was good since Betsy had to close the library and then walk to her car alone.

Nash pulled the Jeep in next to her car and got out.

Taking an ice scraper he cleared off her windows. Then he reached into the back of the Jeep for some cardboard that he flattened out and placed on her front windshield. He got back in his Jeep, opened the card and wrote.

Be careful driving home, sweetie.

Nash.

He put the card in the envelope, sealed it and then taking the card and the rose bud he placed them between the cardboard and the windshield. They'd be safe there when she came out. He smiled to himself, as he got back into his Jeep and drove away.

Thinking of how surprised Betsy would be and how it might light up her smile made him happier than he'd been in weeks. He'd loved to have stayed to surprise her himself but he'd promised to meet Jim and Lance at the gun range tonight.

The practice would be good for them. Their buddy Lance needed to let off some steam, and Nash did too. Plus it wouldn't do to let his skills deteriorate. Eight months out and he'd been lazy, at first, caught up in dealing with the loss of sight in one eye and getting used to the eye patch. He'd felt his life was ruined. Too often in the past eight months, that loss of hope had crept in.

But it wasn't going to win this time. Not now that he had someone to hope for. A sweet, shy librarian who made him smile just thinking about her.

He smiled imagining her reaction to the note and flower.

CHAPTER FOUR

*B*etsy came out of the library and hurried to her car, trying not to slip on the wet parking lot.

At least tonight she didn't have to worry about driving on a bad tire. Her thoughts turned to Nash and how he had been there for her when she needed him. Twice now.

She was dreading the confrontation with Leann when she got home. Playing a parental role was no fun when she just wanted to have a normal relationship with her sister. But that wouldn't happen if Leann was going to act like an irresponsible child.

Her mind on the coming confrontation, she didn't notice the cardboard on her windshield until she was nearly in the car.

"Oh, what is this?" She moved to the front of the car and reached to pull the cardboard off.

Someone was very thoughtful and she had a sneaking suspicion who it was.

Beneath the cardboard was a pink rose bud and a card.

A smile spread across her face.

Nash was here today. It had to be him.

She opened the car door and got inside. Seated behind the wheel, she placed the rose on her dash and opened the envelope.

To a sweet girl, the card said. She opened it.

Who lights up the room.

Beneath he had written, *be careful driving home, sweetie.*

Nash

How thoughtful and sweet. She smiled and her spirits floated with joy at the gift.

Instead of the drive home being one where she focused on the coming confrontation or the memory of that horrible man last night, her thoughts were of Nash and his thoughtfulness.

She parked in the driveway at home and headed into the house calling out, "Hey sis, I'm home."

Leann walked into the living room quieter than usual.

Waiting to be chewed out no doubt.

"How was work?"

"Fine. I'll tell you about it later." She dropped her coat and purse on a chair. "Let's sit down and have a little talk. Then we can figure out where we want to go for dinner."

Leann shrugged. "Fine."

Unable to read her mood, Betsy started in with what she'd planned to say. "Leann, what you did last night was very foolish. First, you got too drunk. Too drunk to be aware of what was going on and that is never safe. Second, you let a man you just met put his hands all over you, probably because you were too drunk to know what you were doing. Do you have any idea how foolish that was and how lucky you are?"

Leann gave her a sheepish look. "Yeah, I know."

"If you do that off campus at one of the bars or at a party something bad could happen and with no one there to stop it. I'm worried about you."

"There's nothing to worry about." Leann shrugged.

"We really haven't talked since you got here, not about the things that matter. How is school? Are your classes hard? Are you passing? Tell me how things are going at school."

"Mostly passing."

"Like you're mostly answering, but not answering." Betsy gave Leann an assessing look. "Tell me what is really going on. Why are you taking this break from school?"

"I just needed a break." Leann shrugged again.

"Why?"

"I just did." Leann frowned, looking away.

"Sis, I can't help you if you won't talk to me."

Silence filled the room and then Leann crossed her arms and spoke. "You won't like hearing this."

"Whatever it is, Leann, I want to know. Please tell me. I just want to help. I just want you to be happy. And downing margaritas and shots as fast as you can, that does not look to me like you are happy."

"There's a guy." Leann looked down at her feet frowning. "If I skip this semester, he will be gone, and I won't have to deal with him anymore."

Betsy was filled with concern. "Has he hurt you? Tell me what's going on."

"He's just kind of creepy. I don't know how else to explain it."

"Start at the beginning."

"We met in algebra class and he asked me out, but I said no because I was going out with another guy. I wasn't doing well in class, so I signed up for tutoring."

"Smart move, sis."

"Well, it didn't help much." Leann shrugged. "Even with the extra sessions. I suck at math."

"You don't suck at math, you just need a good tutor who can explain it and teach it to you."

"Yeah, well, not him because he creeps me out. I had to get away."

"Hold on. Back up." Betsy shook her head at

Leann. "The creepy guy who asked you out and the creepy tutor are they the same person?"

"Yeah. That's who they assigned me. Malcolm Hess. He's one of their tutors but mostly he tutors science."

Betsy frowned. Having tutored English she knew students could request a certain tutor and vice versa. If the guy wanted to spend time with her sister, it was a perfect way to do it. "What a coincidence."

"Yeah. He kept saying how lucky we were to be assigned together."

"And he was in your class?" Betsy watched Leann, but her sister seemed to be missing Betsy's sarcasm or her point. "Kind of strange to be tutoring a subject you are taking yourself, don't you think? I'd say there is more going on there than luck. He could have seen your name on the request list and told them he would tutor you. That could easily happen but to tutor you in the same subject, the same class, when he hasn't even passed it yet. Leann that is more than a little odd. I'm surprised they let him do that."

Leann blinked at her and then her mouth went into an "O" the light dawning. "Well, they did."

"So tell me about this tutoring."

"At first we met at the library." Leann smiled. "Which made me think of you. Every time I go into that library, I think of you working at this one."

Betsy gave her a smile in return. "That's sweet,

sis." She waited a pause and then said, "Go on. About the tutoring."

Leann curled her legs up onto the couch, wrapping her arms around them. "Then Malcolm insisted I had to meet with him at his place because his schedule was so busy, and he had his own studying to do."

"Studying he couldn't do at the library?"

"He always had a good reason."

"Uh huh, I'll bet he did."

"After I went there a couple times, the weirdness started, but I didn't know how weird until later because it was little stuff."

"Like?"

"Like little touches. Brushing against me, leaning close, moving my hair."

"Things tutors don't do. Totally inappropriate. So what did you do?"

"I needed to pass, so I was trying to just get through it. I'd shift away, try not to sit close, stuff like that."

"Did it ever occur to you to just tell him to stop? That you didn't like that?"

"He'd always act like it was accidental, and he was innocent if I even hinted at the subject, so I stopped trying."

"Moving your hair is not accidental."

"I had to miss an appointment one day, and he got testy. Real testy. He settled down after we rescheduled and met, but it was so strange after that. And it got stranger."

"I'm glad you are here now telling me this and not up there by yourself trying to handle this. You do know you could have called me at any time? Told me what was going on? I'd have listened."

"You two never just listen. You tell me what to do."

"I don't tell you what to do. I suggest things and give my opinion."

Leann rolled her eyes and leaned back on the couch. "Like you could ever just listen. Neither of you do."

"I'm listening now. Tell me everything and don't stop till you're done. I won't say another word until then."

Head thrown back, looking at the ceiling Leann went on. "I caught Malcolm looking through my phone one day when I had gone to use his bathroom. He claimed he was just checking the time, but he'd been in my email. And now I think he may have my password because he knew I was planning to come here to visit, and I had never told him. You and me, we'd just started talking about this visit. He thought I should stay there and study."

Betsy reached over, held Leann's hand and squeezed, determined not to say another word until Leann had finished. Leann squeezed back and smiled. It was something they'd done as kids when she was smaller and would be scared. Like when they went through the annual haunted house.

"He was into my personal business and full of opinions about everything I did. What classes to take next, where I should get a job, and negative about some of the things I was doing and people I was going out with. I wanted to end the tutoring but needed to pass the class, so I was stuck with him."

Betsy took a deep breath and sighed, holding back her words. Instead, she would hold this place for her sister and listen.

"Then finals came and I didn't need to meet with him anymore. I thought everything was done. After I got the plane ticket, which was one week after I'd last seen him, he sent me an email and said guess you don't listen. Have a nice flight. I thought he might have my password, and I changed it so he couldn't see them anymore. But then the night after finals, one of my roommates asked me why he was outside late at night watching my window. That freaked me out, and I started paying attention when-ever I left the building. It felt like he was following me. It gave me the creeps."

Leann turned to look at Betsy.

Betsy could see how scared she was. She squeezed Leann's hand again.

"Betsy, I think he's been stalking me."

Betsy nodded.

"Okay, you can talk now. Really. Enough with the

listening. You proved your point. Sis, I got scared. I didn't know what to do."

"Of course you did, honey. He's not right, and what he's been doing to you is wrong. I'm glad you're safe here and not on campus. Have you reported him to the campus police?"

Leann shook her head. "No. I just got scared and came here."

Betsy got up and went to give her sister a hug. The squeeze hold kind of hug that waits for the other person to exhale and feel a bit better. When she felt Leann give the long exhale, she waited another moment, and then let go.

"Thanks, sis."

"I'm just glad you are here and safe. I love you, Leann, and I just want you to be happy and safe. We can figure this out now that you're here."

"Okay." Leann smiled with her eyes tearing up. "I'm sorry about last night."

"Sweetie, you told me that about a thousand times last night. It's all okay. I forgive you. No need to keep saying sorry. All right?"

Leann nodded.

"I do want to talk about your drinking though. You drank an awful lot last night. How often do you go out drinking and do you get that drunk when you go out?"

"No, I don't do that all the time. Last night was different. But I do go out every weekend with the girls. We always get a pitcher of margaritas to share. I really like them. Don't you? You only had one."

"Tequila and I are not fond of each other. But it doesn't matter. Okay. You like margaritas, but why so much last night?"

"He sent me a text right after we got to the bar. Said he hoped I was having a good time and not to drink too much. That freaked me out. I sent back please stop texting me. But I think that made him mad. Because he started blowing up my phone with texts. I could feel it vibrating in the pocket of my jeans, but I wouldn't look at any more of them. I didn't want to look. He was going crazy, and I got scared."

"Leann, why didn't you tell me instead of sucking down drinks like there was no tomorrow? I had no idea this was going on. I was right there. You didn't have to suffer and suck down drinks. You should have told me."

"We were having a good time, and I didn't want to ruin it. I thought coming here, he would stop bothering me. I thought telling him to stop last night would stop it."

"You're going to have to report this to the police, Leann. Can I see the texts?" Betsy held out her hand for Leann's phone.

Leann shook her head. "No. I deleted them this morning. I couldn't stand to look at them."

"I understand that, sweetie, and I hate that this

guy is stalking you. He could be a real nut job. I wish it would all just go away too, but wishful thinking isn't going to make it happen. If he sends you any more texts you've got to save them for evidence. The police will want to see them. If he contacts you in any way from now on, we need a record. Phone calls, texts, emails. Everything he does."

"Okay, sis, I will."

"Good. I'll research stalkers at the library tomorrow and we can educate ourselves on what to do. It's not a subject I know much about. Now, how about we go out for dinner and relax. I think we both need that."

"That sounds good." Leann nodded. "I want you to tell me about that handsome guy who rescued us last night. The one you introduced me to at the library. What was his name?"

"Nash."

"I'd like to thank Nash, if you know how to get a hold of him."

"We can do that." Betsy glanced at her phone. "I know how to reach him, and I need to call him anyway to thank him."

"Ooh, let's call him and invite him out for pizza. That's a good way to thank him. Guys love pizza." Leann was back to her peppy self, and Betsy couldn't help but smile.

It is a good way to thank him. For the other night and for giving me a ride home that icy night.

"Okay. Yes, we can do that."

"Call him. Before he makes other plans."

"Okay. Okay. Don't be so impatient."

Betsy reached for her phone and dialed.

Nash answered on the third ring, out of breath. "Hello, sweet. Everything okay?"

Betsy couldn't help but smile. The way he said those words lit a happy feeling inside of her. "Hello Nash. Yes, everything is fine. Did I catch you at a bad time?"

"Never a bad time for you. I just finished my run. What's up?"

"Well, first I want to thank you for cleaning off my car windows and for the card and flower. It was such a nice surprise."

"You're welcome. I hoped you'd like that."

"Yes, I did. Very much."

"Good. I'm glad."

"The other reason I called is we wanted to invite you out for pizza tonight as a thank you for last night."

There was a pause.

In her nervousness amid the silence, unable to wait another second for him to respond, she blurted out, "But if you're busy or you don't want to…"

"Hold on now. I'm not busy, and I would love to go out for pizza with you. But you don't need to thank me."

"Yes, we do. Leann wants to thank you herself.

Where would you like to go? What's your favorite pizza place?"

"Has your sister been to Memphis Pizza Café in midtown yet?"

"No."

"Then let's take her there."

"Okay, that sounds good."

"I need a shower first."

"I just got home myself. Meet you there in an hour?"

"Sure. Looking forward to it."

"Me too."

Betsy hung up and then glanced at her sister who was giving her that look. "What?" She frowned.

"You like this guy Nash." Leann started grinning. "More than a little."

"Well, he's just been very nice."

"Nah, it's more than that. More than nice." Leann laughed. "Admit it, sis. You think he's hot. And he is. A hot, nice, sexy, hero who saves damsels in distress."

Betsy blushed.

"See. Look at you blushing." Leann laughed.

"Okay, I admit it. I do think he is all those things."

"What's this about a card and flower?"

Betsy detailed the nice surprise she'd found when she came out to her car. She went over to her purse and pulled out the card Nash had left for her and picked up the rose bud. "I need to put this in water."

"Wow sis. Nash is a keeper. Now we just need to get him to ask you out after we have pizza."

"He has already asked me out once."

"Oh! Now who's holding back on who?"

"Well, I said no when he asked."

"Are you crazy? Why would you do that?"

"Because you were coming to town."

"Oh." Leann's eyes widened. "Was he at the Electric Cowboy looking for you?"

"No, I don't think so. I didn't tell him we were going there. It had to be a coincidence. He was there with his buddies."

"Oh well if you say so." Her tone suggested she didn't believe this one bit.

Despite her words, Leann's question and tone had put the doubt in her mind. She would have to ask him how he came to be there just at the moment they needed him.

"Hey, you know his friends were hot too. Maybe if he asked you out again, we could double date."

Betsy didn't answer. A double date with her baby sister and some guy was not her idea of a fun evening. That was not happening.

BETSY AND LEANN walked into the café and saw Nash

seated at a table wearing jeans, a jean shirt and the ever-present black eye patch.

"Wow, sis. He's sexy in a dangerous sort of way. Intense," Leann said.

"Yes, he is."

"I didn't see him that well the other night when he was fighting that guy. It's kind of a blur. But I know he kicked butt. He's really hot, sis."

"You were too drunk. You thought they were all hot."

"And I'll bet they were."

He waved at them, and they walked over to join him.

"Nash, you remember my sister, Leann," Betsy said.

"Yes. Nice to see you again, Leann." He held out his hand, and Leann shook it.

They sat and looked at their menus for a moment, and then Leann said, "What's good, Nash? Which is your favorite pizza?"

"I like the Café Supreme. It comes with mozzarella, Canadian bacon, pepperoni, onion, green pepper, beef, sausage and mushrooms."

"Oh, that sounds good. Let's get that."

"Betsy?" He looked over at her. "What kind would you like?"

"Café Supreme sounds wonderful." She smiled at him, and he smiled back as the waitress arrived.

"What would all y'all like to drink?"

"Pepsi." Leann was a Pepsi drinker, a habit Betsy had given up.

"Water with lemon." Betsy was trying to lose weight so she mostly drank water.

"What have you got on tap?" Nash looked at the waitress.

"Brown Bear."

"Sounds good. I'll have that. And we'd like a fifteen inch Café Supreme."

"Coming right up."

After she walked away Leann said, "Nash, I can't thank you enough for what you did last night. I guess it could have been pretty bad."

"No need to thank me." He shook his head. "Glad I was there."

"And I want to thank you for last night and for helping me with the flat tire earlier," Betsy said. "It was thoughtful of you to clear off my car tonight," she tucked her hair behind her right ear and then glanced down at her napkin, playing with it as she spoke again, her shyness taking over. "And the flower and card were sweet. Thank you."

"Really ladies, I don't need thanked for last night. I was happy to help." He tipped his head trying to capture Betsy's gaze fully. "I hoped you'd like the surprise today. You're welcome."

"Hold on," Leann interrupted what was turning into a more private conversation, "Flat tire?" She looked back and forth from Nash to Betsy. "What happened?"

"Back when we had that ice storm, I came out of the library to head home and had a flat. Nash gave me a ride home." She looked at him and smiled. "That's twice now you've come to the rescue. Thank you."

He smiled back at her. "You are welcome. Any time."

The drinks and the pizza arrived.

Betsy waited until they'd nearly finished eating to bring up Leann's stalker. After Nash had taken a swallow of beer and seemed to be full, she broached the subject. "Nash, there's something I'd like your advice on. There's a situation Leann is dealing with right now, and it may be serious."

"What's up?"

"She has a stalker."

Nash's expression turned serious. "Go on."

She and Leann together explained what was going on while Nash quietly listened.

"This guy Malcolm is a threat. Do either of you carry a gun or a Taser or know self-defense?"

"No, neither of us have taken martial arts or learned self-defense. We don't carry guns, or knives or Tasers. Never been around them. Our family is all girls, and we never really fought even when we were growing up, at least not in a physical way. When that man grabbed hold of Leann, neither of us knew what to do. I'm so glad you were there. Now we have this other problem."

Nash wished he could wipe the worry away from Betsy's pretty green eyes. He wanted to help her sister, but he couldn't help wondering if the girl brought these problems onto herself by the way she acted.

If Leann behaved around other guys like she had last night with the guy from the bar, she was asking for trouble by allowing too many liberties and this guy on campus could be trouble.

"I could teach you both, but what she really needs is a Taser. You don't want to let them get close enough to you to grab you."

"We can look into that. I hadn't thought of a Taser," Betsy said. "Thank you."

" I'd love a self-defense lesson," Leann piped up. "When can you come over and teach us?"

"Tomorrow, after class if you're available then. I can show you some basic moves. But you still need a Taser."

"Oh, good! Betsy will be off work at three-thirty. It's an early day for her."

Leann's cheerful enthusiasm made him smile along with the thought of seeing Betsy once again.

The check came, and Nash automatically reached for it, but Betsy snatched it up before he had it in his hand.

"No, this one is our treat. Our way of saying thank you," Betsy said.

Nash didn't need a thank you, and he wasn't used to women picking up the tab, but he wasn't going to argue with her and create friction between them right now.

She got out her credit card, gave it to the waitress and then said to Nash, "I just have a quick question before we go."

"Okay."

"Were you on your way in to the Electric Cowboy when you saw us or on your way out?"

"On our way out."

"I didn't see you in there."

"We were on the other side of the room. I was planning to ask you to dance. But then you left, and that guy followed you. I didn't like the look of things, so I decided to see that you were okay."

"Oh." Betsy's eyes widened. "So it wasn't a coincidence. You followed us out."

"Yes ma'am, I did." He nodded. "Me and the boys were ready to leave anyway."

"Do you go there often?"

"Nope." He shook his head.

"Why were you there last night?"

"Because I'd suggested it. I overheard Leann mention it to you at the library, and it sounded like fun. Been a long time since I went dancing."

Leann leaned back in the booth, a slight frown on her face.

"I didn't see you out there dancing," Betsy said.

"Well, I'd hoped to be dancing with you. Wasn't anybody else I wanted to ask."

e hoped he'd be dancing with me.

Betsy smiled and blushed.

"I'd like to take you dancing one night," he said. "If you're interested. That, or dinner and a movie. Next weekend?"

"Maybe," Betsy said. "I have to check my work schedule."

Leann had been sitting quietly with that slight frown on her face, but now she spoke. "You were eavesdropping on our conversation, figured out where we were going, and set it up for you and your buddies to be there?"

"You make that sound pretty bad. It wasn't like that. I was at the library looking for a book and just happened to overhear you. The guys had asked if I wanted to get together for a beer and I suggested the Electric Cowboy because I thought it would be fun if

Betsy wanted to dance. I just wanted to ask her to dance, that's all."

"I don't think I believe in bumping into men coincidentally any more. Geez do you all pull this shit?" Leann leaned on the table, scowling at him.

"You're lumping all men in with your stalker." Nash shook his head. "The rest of us aren't like that guy Malcolm. We might want to know where a girl might be in order to talk to her and ask her out, but that's not the same as stalking her. And overhearing someone speaking is not the same as following them around and listening to them."

"Sure sounds like it to me, and I don't want you stalking my sister."

"I am not stalking your sister."

Betsy wasn't sure what to think as she watched and listened while thoughts rang through her head.

It wasn't coincidence. He tried to set it up that we'd bump into each other.

She watched Nash, thoughts running through her head and a frown to match her sister's forming.

Does he have stalker tendencies, too? He gets so angry. The way he was last night. Do I need to be worried about him? Every time something happens he's always right there. Maybe none of that is coincidence. Maybe that's not a good thing. I don't know what to think.

"I suggest you look up stalking before you accuse all men of having those tendencies. And stop directing your anger at me. I hate that you have a stalker, but his name is Malcolm Hess, and I am not him. You have a situation that needs to be dealt with and that's where your attention ought to be right now."

"I'd planned to research this subject tomorrow at work," Betsy spoke very quietly, to diffuse the rising tension between the two. "We're going to figure out a way to deal with this."

"Good. If there's anything I can do to help, let me know."

"Thank you. And thank you again for stepping up to help me and my sister."

Nash nodded his head. "You're welcome."

Betsy stood and as they gathered their coats and got ready to go, thoughts continued running through her head. Back and forth like ping-pong. Her attraction to Nash and the way he took care of things making sure she and her sister were safe along with the heroic qualities in him on one side and on the other, the fierceness and violence she'd seen in him when he pulled his knife on that guy outside the Electric Cowboy and had him down on the ground and now the possibility he was watching her and following her. Overwhelmed by all her conflicting thoughts and feelings about Nash, she just wanted to go home and think.

Is he telling the truth when he says he wasn't following me? I just don't know him well enough. I'd like to get to know him better, but not if he has stalking and controlling tendencies. I'd love to go dancing, or to dinner and a movie with him. But I can't say yes right now. I need to know he's okay to go out with first, and right now I need to focus on my sister more than anything else.

Nash watched the Bobbins sisters walk away and asked himself if dating Betsy would be a mistake. Drama, the real kind of drama seemed to follow her because of her sister. *Would it stop or would there always be something?* He wasn't sure he'd be up to another girlfriend who brought the drama. If he got a date with her, that is.

Getting Betsy to go on a first date was turning into a challenge. And her sister wasn't helping things. Even at this thank you dinner the girls had initiated, Betsy's sister was stirring up drama by accusing him of stalking her sister.

Normally, Nash liked a challenge. He just wasn't sure he was ready for this one. But ready or not, Betsy was the one. The more time he spent near her, the more that feeling grew. She was the sweet girl he wanted to be going out with. Patience and persistence meant winning, so he'd give all he had and hope for the best.

BETSY WAS at the library hovering over her computer screen, looking up facts on stalking when June stopped behind her and leaned over her shoulder. "What are you so intent on? Must be good."

"I'm researching stalking. Listen to this. 'One in six women and one in nineteen men have experienced stalking victimization during their lifetime in which they felt very fearful or believed that they or someone close to them would be harmed or killed. Persons aged eighteen to twenty-four years experience the highest rate of stalking.' And it's a problem on college campuses. I had no idea."

"I didn't either. Your sister is on campus. Is that the reason you're looking this up? Is Leann in trouble?"

"Yes, she is, and that is why I'm looking into it."

"Oh, no."

"I thought she was doing fine. But she's not and I just found out about it the other night. Now, I'm wishing she was going to school closer to one of us."

"I can understand that. Maybe she could transfer to the University of Memphis."

"Eighty percent of campus stalking victims know their stalker. The guy who has been stalking her was her algebra tutor."

"Oh, wow. He wasn't her professor was he? Because you could have him fired."

"No, he's another student. And he must have pulled something because he was in the same class with her that he was tutoring her for. That's not normal."

"Wow. No, it's not."

"I'm trying to figure out what exactly we can do about this guy."

"Right. Good plan."

"One study shows about a third of students on campus have been stalked during their lifetimes. College campuses are an ideal environment for stalkers since they are relatively closed-in communities where daily routines and regular behaviors can easily be monitored. More importantly–both stalkers and their victims are measurably more intelligent than average. The higher intelligence of stalkers accounts for their resourceful and manipulative skills when their intelligence is misdirected."

"Great. That probably means they are harder to catch."

"She just wants him to stop, but I don't think he's going to unless the police get involved. He was texting her the other night when we went out. Even after she asked him to stop. "

"Oh wow, so he wasn't just following her around campus? If he kept it up while she's here... oh hey, and didn't she skip this semester to take some time off?"

"Yes, she did."

"She's not in classes and she's not on campus, but he's still harassing her?"

Betsy nodded.

"Betsy that does not sound good."

"I don't think there's anything good about these kinds of guys. They list the different types of stalkers on this site, but really we don't know enough about Malcolm Hess to know just how dangerous he is. He could be a real nut job. I'd feel better if Leann came to live with me."

"Will she do that?"

"I don't know, but I'm going to ask her tonight."

"I know how much you must worry about her going back to campus."

"Yes, I do."

"I hope she says yes."

"Me too."

LEANN HAD MADE spaghetti for dinner and the scent hovered in the air.

Betsy walked in the front door, took a breath and said, "It smells delicious."

"I made spaghetti. Thought it would be a nice surprise."

"It is very sweet of you, sis. Thank you. Did you make it like mom used to?"

"Yes, except I added those mushrooms you had in the fridge."

"Yum. I could get used to this. Want to move in?" Betsy took off her coat and hung it up.

Leann laughed. "You just want a live in cook."

Betsy walked into the kitchen. "Yes, that would be nice. But we'd take turns."

" I'm not a great cook. Only know how to make three dinners."

"What are they?"

"Spaghetti, chili and tacos. Those are good feed a date dinners. Guys like them."

"True. Yes, they would. Do you cook for your dates often?"

"Not often. Only if he makes it to the third date and I still like him."

Betsy got out plates and silverware to set the table. Leann stirred the sauce again.

Once they were seated and ready to eat, Betsy brought up the subject again. "Sis, about moving in with me. Why don't you look into the University of Memphis? You could transfer and instead of living on campus, live here. The only thing is, you couldn't throw parties. I need to relax after work and get a good night's sleep. If you think you could handle a quieter lifestyle, I'd love to have you here."

"I don't throw parties now. The girls and I go out to the bars."

"You'd miss your friends, I know, but you'd make new friends."

"And you wouldn't worry about me if I was here, where you would know what was going on. That's what's really going on here. I can take care of myself, sis. You know, do things for myself like a grownup?"

Betsy sighed. The conversation was taking a turn she wanted to avoid. Too many times in the past Leann had been more of a baby sister than Betsy would have liked, all while complaining her sisters weren't giving her enough space. If she'd behaved more like an adult, they'd have treated her more like one. "I know you can. And I do worry about you, but this isn't about me, Leann. I just want you to be safe."

"I'll think about it."

"Okay, good."

"What did you find out at the library? Did you do any research?"

"I did. And did you get out your laptop and do some research too?"

"No. You're better at research than I am."

And this is why we don't recognize your independence. Because you aren't behaving like an independent woman. Instead of doing things for yourself you wait for other people to do things for you.

That's what she'd like to have said to her sister, and they would have to have that talk soon. But right now she was cutting her some slack so they could focus on the main problem. Malcolm Hess.

"I found out a lot. This is not an isolated thing. A lot of girls on college campuses have been victims of stalking. You are far from alone."

"Wow. I had no idea."

"Neither did I." Betsy shook her head. "You could have called the campus police and made them aware. But you should never confront your stalker because some of them can become very angry. It's better to have someone else, like the police, do it."

"Okay, I messed up there."

"It's okay to say stop calling or texting me. It's okay to say that and to say no to them, but you don't want to confront them. Just firmly say no and leave no gray area so it is very clear."

"I did tell him."

"Has he called you or texted you today?"

"I don't know. I kept my phone turned off."

Betsy eyed her sister. "It's real nice that you cooked dinner for us and the spaghetti is delicious."

"Thanks, sis."

"But did you leave the house today?"

Leann shook her head.

"You had your phone turned off. Did you get online?"

"No."

"You didn't leave the house, didn't use your phone or computer." What she'd suspected was true. "You're afraid to."

Leann shrugged. "Maybe a little."

"You're safe here, Leann. You're a day's drive away from campus. It's okay for you to go outside, go shopping, anything else you want to do. It's okay to turn your phone on and to check emails."

"Yeah, I know. I just wanted a day away from everything. All the electronics, people, you know?"

"I know. And you made mom's spaghetti."

"Yeah."

"Comfort food."

"Yeah."

"After we eat why don't you turn on your phone and check email messages. If he's still trying to get in touch with you, we need to start saving them for the police to see. And don't you want to see if you have any messages from your friends?"

"Yeah, I do, and I will. After we eat."

"Okay, let's enjoy this yummy spaghetti and talk about something else for a little bit. Some of our library patrons are real characters. Let me tell you about Mrs. Verte. She called three times today." Betsy grinned.

If she had to deal with Mrs. Verte and her poisonous frogs and lizards, at least it made for entertaining dinner conversation. Mrs. Verte had now added frogs to the list of imagined poisonous creatures who could kill her in Florida. *It was always going to be something with her.* She'd at least stopped talking about the lizards.

They laughed over the silly woman and then, done with their dinner, cleared the table and put the dishes in the dishwasher.

"Okay, I'm headed for a lavender salts bath. My feet are killing me," Betsy said. "I'm going to take a soak. When I get done, you can tell me what you found out about your messages, if there are any."

"Okay, sis. Enjoy your bath."

"Thanks." Betsy smiled and headed down the hallway as Leann got out her laptop and fired it up.

When Betsy came back into the living room in her big terrycloth robe, Leann looked up from her computer.

"I looked up the programs at the University of Memphis. I could transfer here. Not sure how long that would take."

"You could call them tomorrow and ask."

"Yeah, that's a good idea. Or I could go down there. Check into it. Look the campus over."

Good. That would get her out of the house and doing something proactive and productive instead of hiding away here.

"I've only been there for a couple of their theater productions. I don't know the campus well. Otherwise I'd offer to take you around."

"It's okay, sis. I'll enjoy exploring by myself. You've been taking me around and entertaining me since I got here. I've enjoyed it, but I can do this on my own."

"Sounds like a plan. You can borrow my car. Oh, a couple more things to put on your to do list. Change the passwords on all your accounts if you think he got into your password. Whether he did or he didn't, I think it would be a good idea to change passwords on everything you have to a new one you have never used before. It's one of the things they say to do if you have a stalker."

"Yeah, okay. I can do that."

"Has he sent you any messages?"

"No, not today."

Her phone chose that moment to chime with a new text. Leann looked at it, turned pale and handed her sister the phone.

Malcolm's text read, *Mr. Whiskers misses you. Better come home soon.*

Beneath the text was a picture of a small white kitten on a red collar and leash.

"He has Mr. Whiskers," Leann whispered, fear in her eyes.

Betsy looked at the phone and frowned and then said, "Wait. You have a cat?"

"Yeah, he just showed up on the back steps one day, hungry and mewing."

"Where is Mr. Whiskers now?"

"I don't know," Leann whispered and then closed her eyes. "He doesn't have a leash. I think Malcolm has my kitty."

"Don't answer him. I know you are worried about your kitty, but don't answer him. That's what he wants."

"I don't know what to do."

"Who was supposed to be feeding Mr. Whiskers? Can you contact them?"

"Yeah, I can do that." Leann took her phone back and sent a message to her roommate Chloe.

How is Mr. Whiskers doing? Have you checked on him lately?

Chloe texted back. *I'm out of town for two days. You told me he'd be okay for a couple days on his own as long as he had food and water.*

Okay, thanks. Let me know how he is when you get back. Leann sent the message. Then she turned to Betsy who was quietly waiting to hear.

"Bets, I don't know where he is. My roommate went out of town for a couple of days and left him." She handed over her phone for her sister to check the texts.

Betsy read them and then handed the phone back. "Okay, try not to worry. This guy may just be messing with you and mean the kitten no harm. That pic might not even be of Mr. Whiskers. It could be some other kitten that Malcolm is using a pic of to draw you out since you went silent on him."

But even as she said it, Betsy doubted her own words. The research she had done told her that a stalker sometimes went after the person's pet when they couldn't get at the person. Things did not look good for Mr. Whiskers.

"Tomorrow I want you to call the campus police and tell them what is going on. There's nothing more we can do tonight."

Betsy received a text of her own when her phone chirped.

Nash.

Should I come over right after you get off work or do you want a little time to unwind before your lesson?

I can't deal with that right now. I'll call you some other time. She sent the message back and then gave her full attention to her sister who was talking.

"Maybe you are right. Maybe he doesn't have Mr. Whiskers. I hope he doesn't. Damn it, I should have brought him with me. I just didn't think you'd want a kitten in the house. He gets into everything and sometimes he stays up all night making noises."

"You could have brought him. It would have been okay. And he can live here too. Even if he is a noisy night owl." Betsy smiled at her sister hoping to ease her mind.

"Thanks, sis. I know you need to get to bed because you have work tomorrow."

"Yes, I do. Are you going to be okay? Try not to let this keep you up all night if you can help it."

"I'll try."

Betsy went to bed wondering if she would sleep knowing what she knew about stalkers. Malcolm Hess. Even his name gave her the creeps, and she didn't even know the guy. Now he had her sister's cat. She was sure of it. She just hoped he didn't mistreat the sweet little thing.

If he was an animal abuser or an animal killer,

that made him a more dangerous stalker. The kind that could really hurt her sister.

Leann was awake long into the night.

Just how crazy is this guy, and what might he do to her sister or to her sister's sweet little kitten?

CHAPTER SIX

*N*ash, after receiving her message, decided Betsy didn't want a lesson in self-defense and didn't want him coming around. What else was he to think from the way she had just put him off? What did she mean she "can't deal with that"? Then "I'll call you." If that wasn't a brush off, he didn't know what was.

Betsy was blowing hot and cold. It was too much to keep up with and reminded him too much of his ex, Nicole.

Nicole had started out sweet too. Sweet as the piece of pecan pie they'd shared the first time they met. Her insisting they could share the last slice the café had for sale had been what brought them together. He'd found her southern charm and those innocent big blue eyes irresistible. It wasn't long until they went from dating to engaged. She was thrilled to be engaged to a Marine. Until he was shipped overseas and she didn't have his attention almost every day. That was when she started blowing hot and cold. With Nicole, it was always about Nicole.

Betsy wasn't like Nicole in that way. She wasn't self-centered and she cared about others, especially her sister. And that was a problem now because Leann had obviously taken a sudden dislike to him.

Well, he wasn't a damn stalker, and he would give Betsy space, plenty of it until she figured that out. He had things to do like finish his own degree, go to his VA appointments and finish working on his Harley. Now that the frame was in, he had a lot of work to do reassembling the bike. Which was good because it would help keep his mind off the pouty little librarian and her kissable red lips.

Her reaction still irked him.

Her sister was inviting all this drama by her behavior, and if the two sisters didn't want his help, there was nothing he could do about it.

If Leann had not come to town, he and Betsy would have been on their first date by now, getting to know each other better. But she had come to town, so now this was how it was.

His head had started to pound again. A real life situation to deal with, not a self-inflicted drama. He should be the one saying; I can't deal with that right now.

I have my own problems to deal with right now.

He put his phone away and glanced in the mirror at his scarred eye socket.

What woman would want to look at that?

Even if Betsy did go out with him, even if they became close, close enough for him to remove the eye patch, what she saw when he took it off would scare her away.

Maybe this is for the best. If we never get started, never move this beyond a friendship level, that's probably best for both of us.

His head now pounding he closed his eyes and laid back on his bed.

Damn headaches.

He could tackle the world if not for these damn headaches. Best he stayed away from her anyway, when he was like this.

NASH'S LIBRARY books were already two weeks late when he went back to the library to return them. He stacked them under his arm, locked his Jeep and headed for the door, nervous about how Betsy would react to seeing him.

He'd been avoiding Betsy while he battled the headaches, knowing he was not a pleasant man to be around and not wanting her to see him or hear him as a growling bear when he was in pain. The headaches had come back strong as ever along with dreams that woke him in the middle of the night and left him tired and frustrated the next day. It had taken a while to get them under control.

She'd called the first week to tell him his books were overdue, and he hadn't called her back.

He'd replayed her message three times in the middle of the night just to hear her voice, something he'd never been likely to do before meeting her. Her voice had a calming effect on him, but finally after the third time, disgusted with himself, he deleted it off his phone.

He'd also been in the VA for a week while they did a sleep study among other things. Adjusting his meds had brought the headaches back under control and allowed him to sleep again. The dreams had stopped again and he felt more like himself.

She'd called this morning, and he went over that conversation in his head.

"Nash? This is Betsy. Are you all right?"

"I'm fine. Why?"

"Well, you haven't been in for a while. I was just concerned about you."

"I'm fine."

So she did care. Enough to check on him and ask.

"Did you know your audio books are overdue?"

"Yes."

"Oh."

"I've been busy."

"I see."

Her tone indicted that she really didn't, and he realized he was being more like that growling bear than he should be toward her. Maybe if he dropped by the library and returned the books they could talk. He'd at least get to see her again.

"I can drop them by. You working now?"

"Yes, I am."

"I'll see you later today."

"Oh, good." Her voice had sounded as if she'd be happy to see him.

It was encouraging, but he didn't want to get too pumped up about it. Otherwise there could be the letdown.

He carried the books in wondering what her reaction to seeing him again would be. Not used to explaining himself to anyone and never one to make excuses, he wouldn't tell her why he hadn't called her back, now that she'd called again. Though he probably should have apologized for ignoring her and explained why.

He wondered how her sister was and hoped the guy they'd told him about had backed off. He hoped Leann had just been exaggerating the way drama queens do.

Walking in the door he saw Betsy standing with her back to him, arranging the books on a round table by the entrance where the new books were usually displayed. He approached quietly so as not to startle her.

Her long blonde hair hung down her back, and he took in her curves. A long sleeved blue dress hugged her curves as she leaned forward and those black suede boots beneath, which were no good in snow, made him smile as he remembered driving her home the night of the ice storm.

Then she straightened and turned and looked up at him, her eyes widening in surprise.

"Nash," she said as her whole face lit up.

It warmed him clear to his bones and dashed away the doubts that had been hovering. She was happy to see him. Of that he had no doubt.

"Betsy," he said her name and smiled.

She was glad to see him just as he had hoped. In fact, she seemed as if she held her breath, her green eyes lit and her smile grew wider. Her eyes were drinking him in as if she were thirsty for the sight of him.

Taking a break from each other had only increased the attraction between the two of them. He stepped closer carrying his books, each step building the current between them. Their gazes locked upon each other.

He smiled and said, "I believe I owe you some fines for these."

She smiled in return. "Yes, you do. And I believe I owe you an apology."

"For?"

Sweet, sweet Betsy. What could she want to apologize for? Could it be that she was sorry she hadn't trusted him?

He dared to hope for that much.

IT HAD BEEN two weeks since she'd seen Nash. Long enough to figure out he was no stalker. He'd dropped her like a hot potato, and now she felt bad for having ever thought he was one, and for her sister going off on him the way she had. He'd done nothing but protect them and be a nice guy and, pizza or not, look how she'd treated him. It had been eating at her.

Her sister was paranoid, and she shouldn't have listened to her.

And she'd missed Nash. Why, she didn't know. They'd never even gone out once, but she missed him.

Innocent until proven guilty. She hadn't given him that much.

Has he been avoiding me? Is that why he didn't bring his library books back? Why he didn't return my call? Or has it been something else? Maybe the PTSD he'd hinted at. Maybe he hasn't been feeling well. I've been reading up on eye injuries and know a little bit more about them now. I wonder how much of his moodiness could be attributed to his injuries.

Whatever it was, she couldn't ask him. Not after the way she'd brushed him off before. She'd been trying to reach out to him again with the phone calls. As she'd told Leann, he was obviously not a stalker, and she didn't want to hear any more about that.

Leann was seeing stalkers in every corner, which was ridiculous.

When Betsy saw Nash again, she could only express that she had missed him and was glad to see him again.

When he walked in the door, he took her breath away. He'd cut his hair, and it was now shaped around his head instead of hanging down where it sometimes hung in front of his eye patch like a shield.

Wow, he looks good. So handsome and rakish with the patch and that new haircut. He enters the room and you can't help but look at him.

The intensity from before was reigned in. He approached her with his books under his arm. "I believe I owe you some fines for these."

"Yes, you do. And I believe I owe you an apology."

"For?"

"For mistrusting, for believing you could be a

bad guy and for pushing you away instead of talking with you about it."

"Well, that's a good start. What do I owe you?"

She rattled off the fine, and he paid it.

Afraid he would just go when she didn't want him to, she pressed on. "I hope I am forgiven for thinking the worst of you. It was wrong of me. And after you had helped us so much. It must have felt like a slap in the face."

His clear eye took her in as he listened, and then he said, "Sweetheart, it was a low blow, but I'm a big guy and I can take more than my fair share of shit that's dished out. Don't worry about it. I'm over it."

And over me, more than likely. But I don't want you to be.

"I, I ..." there she went again with the incomplete sentences. Her words stuck in her throat. "I would love to go to dinner with you." Her voice dropped low, and she couldn't hold his gaze. "If you still wanted to, that is."

"Betsy, you can wind me around your bobbin any day."

She looked up at him suddenly feeling lifted like a balloon and giggled.

"I've been saving that one for a long time. Wasn't sure I'd ever get to use it. Thought you'd be happier if I went away."

"Harrumph," Mrs. Geraldine E. Watson made

the noise behind Nash. "If you two are done googly eyeing each other."

Betsy's jaw dropped.

"Set the date already. Some of us have books to be checked out."

"Yes, ma'am." Betsy reached for the books as Nash stepped aside.

"Tonight?" he asked.

"Yes, tonight is good."

"What time are you off?"

"Five-thirty."

"Pick you up at six-thirty?"

"Yes." Betsy nodded.

"It's a date." He grinned and it nearly lit up the room.

Betsy just wanted to stand staring after him, but Mrs. Watson was tapping her shoe against the floor and waiting impatiently.

Googly eying each other. Yes, we were. Betsy held back her giggle. She checked out Mrs. Watson while trying not to watch Nash walk out the door.

HE PULLED up out front in his Jeep, and Betsy stopped alternating between pacing and peering out the living room window watching for him.

"I haven't known you to be this nervous on a date

since you were in high school," Leann said. "I've never seen you change clothes so many times."

Five dresses later, Betsy was now wearing a dark red dress. The one she'd never worn anywhere but had bought for a special occasion. A someday.

The deep red silk hugged her body and showed off her legs. She even had red shoes to match, and of course the perfect shade of lipstick.

"Don't worry, sis," Leann said. "You look hot. He won't be able to keep his eyes or his hands off of you."

"He's here." Butterflies were in her belly, and it wasn't just that she was hungry. In fact, she wondered if she would be too nervous to eat.

Why are first dates often dinner dates anyway? There is so much pressure on a first date and on a first kiss. First kisses. What will kissing him be like?

Then he was at the door, and she was opening it, feeling like a schoolgirl again with the first date jitters.

She opened the door. "Hello."

He stood holding a bouquet of three pink and three red roses mixed with white baby's breath.

"Oh, how pretty."

"Hello." He smiled down at her, and his gaze drank her in from her eyes to her lips to her dress. "Not nearly as pretty as you. You look great. Are you almost ready?"

"Yes." Her belly chose that moment to growl.

He laughed. "I was going to ask if you were hungry. But I guess we know the answer to that. What are you hungry for?"

You.

The word popped into her head, but thankfully not out of her mouth where it would have surprised both of them. It had surprised her enough.

"Invite the man in, sis. Geeze," Leann said. "It's cold outside."

"Oh. Yes. Right." She opened the door and stepped back. "Come on in."

Nash stepped inside, his expression still laughing. "Hey Leann. How are you doing?"

"I'm good. Nice to see you, Nash. Make sure my sister has a good time. She doesn't get out much. Spends too much time with her books."

Betsy was taking him in as he talked to her sister. He was wearing a black shirt and black pants, that new haircut, and he was freshly shaved, no shadow showing. He looked so good, she couldn't take her eyes off of him. She wanted to run her hands through his hair and beneath the collar of his shirt before she started to unbutton it.

"I will do my best." He turned back to Betsy before her thoughts carried her completely away. He handed her the flowers.

"I need to put these in water." She spoke the words automatically, but still she stood there, her thoughts elsewhere, lost in the moment and in how handsome he looked.

Leann stood and said, "Here, I'll do that for you."

Betsy handed her the flowers without looking at her. "Thanks, sis."

Nash's gaze held her there, as still as a deer and then he spoke. "We still haven't established what you are hungry for."

Oh my. You might not have, but I have. But oh, he means for dinner. Not afterward. Would there be an afterward?

For the first time in her life she wanted there to be, and on the first date. Which is why she'd let Leann talk her into wearing the sexy red dress. But she needed to answer him, not get lost in a fantasy of how she wanted the evening to go. He stood patiently waiting for her answer.

"Oh, I don't know. Anything except Mexican."

My stomach can't handle Mexican the way it is feeling right now.

"Okay, no Mexican. So Italian, Chinese, Japanese steak house, American, Thai or Vietnamese? Any of those sound good?"

"There's a Vietnamese place downtown that I like, but I've only been there twice with June."

"Saigon Lee?"

"That's the one."

"Good choice. Saigon Lee it is."

"Great." She smiled and reached for her coat. He

helped her put it on, a gesture she liked. It had been a while since she'd been on a date and had a man helping her with coat and doors, doing those gentlemanly things. She'd missed that. Maybe she was in the world of books a bit too much. "See you later, sis."

"Stay out as long as you like. I won't wait up."

"Thanks." Betsy wanted to roll her eyes. Leann was likely hoping Betsy would do the same thing when Leann went out. Well, she was of age. But right now her sister was just being silly. Betsy never stayed out til the wee hours. She was usually home early, curled up with a book.

Nash opened the door of the Jeep for her and helped her climb in. Wearing the high heels and a shorter skirt length, she appreciated the help and the way he checked out her legs.

"I love that dress. It matches your sexy lips."

"I bought lipstick to match the dress."

"Funny. I'd have thought it worked the other way around. Those kissable red lips of yours." He leaned in and lightly brushed her lips with a soft kiss. Then just as his kiss made her want to sigh and relax into more kissing, he pulled away with a smile and closed the door.

There will be kissing. We haven't even made it to dinner yet. And already there is kissing. This sweet as a floating cloud heavenly brush of a kiss which has me feeling like I'm floating on a cloud.

~

THE SMILE on her face showed contentment. Nash was glad he had kissed her.

As he started the car, the radio came on and he turned it down low from where he'd been rocking out on the way over. Rocking out because at last he had a date with this beautiful woman he couldn't get off his mind. He'd even been having romantic dreams about her. Not the usual hot, steamy sex dreams he sometimes had of women, but sweet, slow and sensual dreams. She'd entered his dream life and his life in a way that was different than anyone before.

"How is your sister doing?" He wanted to get the serious talking over so their dinner could be lighter conversation.

"She's doing well. She's decided to transfer to the University of Memphis, and she'll stay with me for the first year. She could stay until she graduates or as long as she wants but she thinks she might want her own place after a while."

"That's good to hear. That way you can keep an eye on her and keep her out of trouble. Her stalker isn't bothering her anymore?"

"I wouldn't say that. She's just handling it better now that she has something to focus on. Something she can control. He is still a very big problem."

"What's he been doing?"

"It's pretty bad, Nash. He's got us both worried. He has her kitten, Mr. Whiskers, but there's no way to get the kitten back, short of going up there which is what I think he's counting on. He keeps texting her and she keeps documenting them, now that she knows to do that, while avoiding answering him."

Son of a bitch. I knew I should have checked in on them. Made sure everything was okay. Instead I let her drive me off to prove a point. Damn it. That was a mistake.

"I wish you had called me."

"What would you have done?"

Gone up there and kicked the guy's ass, but you probably don't want to hear that.

"At the very least I would have listened. Then we could have made a plan to make the guy go away."

"She did tell the campus police and made a report. It's on record now. If he tries anything."

"Good. Was this before or after he took her cat?"

"After. The problem is she can't prove it's her cat, and he is swearing it's his because she gave it to him to keep and then moved out of town. The fact she is transferring appears to them to bear this out. He's lying and they are believing him, not her."

Nash's jaw flexed. "I could go get the cat and have a little talk with him. Make sure he doesn't bother her again."

She sat silently watching his profile.

He felt her looking but didn't want to turn to face

her, so he concentrated on his driving. The last thing he wanted to see right now was fear or revulsion in her eyes.

Damn it. This was not the way this date needs to go. We aren't even at the restaurant yet.

"Good thing the police are on it." He spoke when she said nothing.

"Yes, I'm glad she finally called them. She was too afraid to do that at first."

"I'm glad, too. It was the smart thing to do. Leann will be fine, and the guy will have to accept she has moved out of his reach. He'll find some other girl to latch onto. I'm sorry about the cat."

"Me too. I've seen the pictures, and Mr. Whiskers is an adorable white kitty. He showed up on her back porch one day. Such a sweet fur baby. She hadn't had him long, but I know she got attached nonetheless. She has a thing for kittens. Posts them all over her Facebook page. But she doesn't post anything on there anymore. She doesn't want people like Malcolm to be able to find out things about her. Says it's like living in a fish bowl. I agree. I don't even have a Facebook account."

"That's smart. She has to be careful what she puts out there. I had an account. It's probably still there, but it's been over a year since I logged in."

"Wow. Why did you quit?"

"My ex Nicole was into all that. Posting pics of us, pics of her. She was all about the selfie. She posted new profile pics every day. I haven't been on since this." He pointed to his eye patch. "She wouldn't have her picture taken with me after I got this."

"Oh. I understand. That wasn't very nice of her. I don't think you're missing anything though, not being on social media all the time."

"No, I'm not."

"Though as far as pictures go, I think you look quite dashing with your eye patch. I'd love to have a picture of you and me. We can take one tonight if it's okay with you." She beamed at him, clearly excited at the idea.

God, he loved this woman. She shone light into his dark corners brightening and lightening everything. Not even remotely like Nicole.

Where had Betsy been all his life? Walking around with her nose stuck in a book more than likely. He wished he'd found her sooner. Before he'd lost an eye.

"Is there anything else you'd like to tell me about Leann's stalker? Anything you're worried about or on your mind?"

"No, not right now. Right now I am just looking forward to dinner." She smiled at him and he smiled back as he pulled into the parking lot at Saigon Lee.

"All right. Let's go in and enjoy dinner."

They were seated in a booth and pondering the menu when she placed her menu down and started watching the fish in the tank by the front door.

He put his menu down. "Penny for your thoughts."

"I'm a little over dressed for this restaurant." She pulled her dress down, tugging at the short skirt.

"You could always take it off."

Giggles erupted from that kissable mouth and her whole face lit with laughter.

Good. He'd lightened the mood, which was what they both needed. He loved knowing he could make her laugh like that.

"Not here, silly."

"Okay, not here." He smiled at her.

BETSY'S MIND was now on taking the dress off. And on taking his shirt off. She needed to focus on something else before her thoughts carried her away. She needed to get to know him, not throw off their clothes and get naked.

Though she wanted to. She really, really wanted to. *Getting naked sounded so good right now.*

She knew he wanted to kiss her again by the way his gaze kept dropping to her lips. She couldn't wait for him to kiss her again. The thought made her smile, and he watched every nuance of her face missing nothing.

"Dollar for your thoughts," he said.

"A dollar? Last time it was a penny," she said, surprised.

"Some thoughts are worth more." His gaze searched hers. "And I'd really love to know what you were thinking about just then."

"I was thinking that I hoped you would kiss me again." She blushed. "And often."

"Sweetheart, I'd love nothing more than to wear that lipstick off and send you home knowing you'd been thoroughly kissed."

She smiled wide.

"In fact, come here." He patted the seat beside him.

She stood and he stood to let her scoot in to the inside of the seat. Once she was seated he sat next to her.

"I like this better," he said. "Having you closer."

Blushing she said quietly, "I like this too."

"Still want me to kiss you?"

Giggling she said, "Mmhm."

He put his arm around her and leaned in for a kiss as she turned toward him.

As their lips met she closed her eyes.

Yes, this.

This was what she wanted. What she'd wanted ever since she met him. There was a physical attraction between them that was undeniable. She relaxed into the kiss, the warmth of his lips on hers, the way he tasted, his scent.

This was bliss.

Then the waitress came to take their order, and he broke away one second before the woman spoke. "Are you ready to order?"

She seemed not to be in a very good mood but maybe it was because they were making out in the booth like teenagers.

"Yes," he said.

"Do you like the egg and spring rolls?" he asked Betsy.

"Oh, yes. Those are my favorite things here."

"We'll have one order of spring rolls to share," he told the waitress and then he waited for Betsy to order.

She ordered the very same soup he was going to order.

He laughed. "Apparently we have the same taste in food." He returned his attention to the waitress. "I'll have the same thing."

The woman nodded and walked away.

"I don't think she cared for us kissing in here," Betsy whispered.

"I don't care what she thinks," Nash whispered in her ear. "You taste delicious."

Warmth had risen all through Betsy's body with that kiss and his words sent another type of warmth coursing through her, making her feel sexy and desirable.

The egg rolls came out quickly and they each

wrapped an egg roll in the green lettuce provided and dipped it into the sauce.

Betsy closed her eyes and bit into hers. It was that good.

When she opened her eyes, he was watching her, his gaze dark with desire. "Keep eating like that and you'll make me want to take that dress off right here."

Her eyes widened. "Like what?"

"Like this." He dipped the egg roll, put the end in his mouth, closed his eyes and made an "mmm" sound which sounded so sexy. The actions, sight and sounds mimicked oral sex, which had not even occurred to her when she tasted it.

"Oh!" She opened her eyes wider. "I didn't know I looked and sounded like that. I was just enjoying."

"Well, please don't do that again. I don't think I can take it. Those sexy red lips of yours wrapped around..." He took a deep breath as if gaining control again. "It's not fair to tease a man like that."

"Oh, no." She gave a frowning pout. "I didn't mean to do that. Not at all. I won't do it again."

"Good. Unless you plan to follow through."

"Yes, this is supposed to be a first date, a getting to know you kind of date. I'll try to behave myself."

"Just until we're done with dinner, sweetheart. Then you can have your wild way with me."

My wild way. The thought made her giggle. *What would I do with him if I could have my wild way?*

Nash couldn't wait to find out what would happen after dinner. He could see the wheels turning in Betsy's head and understood that she was both embarrassed by what she thought was forward behavior and tantalized by the thoughts of doing whatever she wanted with him sexually. Something that was obviously new to her.

She was a tantalizing mix herself, of quiet, shy librarian and naughty minded sex kitten. That red dress, her curves and her pouty red lips were enough to drive any man wild.

But he needed to slow things down.

She was his dream girl and he wanted this to last. He didn't want to scare her away, and having sex too fast, too soon, could do that.

There was no reason they couldn't make out hot and heavy, and he'd really like to make sure she was satisfied. When she was happy and he took her home again he'd ask her out on a second date.

Though, if she wanted to go all wild sex kitten on him, he'd let her. To a point.

He was surprised some other guy hadn't snatched her up, but from what Leann had said, Betsy didn't date much. Betsy read books and worked at the library. That was all she did that he knew of. He wondered what hidden depths were there, what desires.

"What do you like to do when you're not at work among the books? Besides reading at home?"

"Sometimes I'll catch a movie, or go to the Brooks Museum of Art, or the Botanic Gardens. When the weather is nice, I'll plant flowers. They always have a plant sale in the spring."

"You like flowers?" He was reminded of his original plan to woo her, one flower at a time. Before her sister and her sister's stalker diverted everyone's attention. He hoped the sister didn't bring a lot of drama into Betsy's home.

"Yes, I love flowers. All kinds."

"Do you have a favorite?"

"No, not really. Most women would say roses, but that is not mine. Though I love the ones you surprised me with. It was sweet of you, and they are beautiful. I like simple flowers like daisies, and exotic flowers like orchids. I'm not sure which one

I'd pick as a favorite if I had to pick one. I like them all."

"Do you have a favorite color?"

"Yes, red and pink." She laughed. "I guess I can't pick just one of those either."

"That's okay. You don't have to pick. I guessed well with your bouquet tonight then."

"Yes, you did." She beamed at him. "They are lovely. Thank you. Now it's my turn. What is your favorite color?"

"Red. Dark red."

"Oh! Another thing we have in common along with the food here."

He smiled. "You look mighty fine in that red dress."

"Thank you. What is your favorite flower?"

He started laughing. No woman had ever asked him that before.

Did men have favorite flowers?

Her eyes were dancing, and he guessed she wasn't all that serious.

He leaned in and whispered in her ear. "I like the way a woman unfolds, opening like a flower, those moist soft petals waiting to be touched with my tongue."

She blushed red as a rose, the blush spreading down her body, her breath changed and in that moment, he knew she would be getting aroused if she hadn't been already.

He had not lost his touch with women. He'd only lost the desire to chase them all. Instead, he wanted his dream girl. The one now sitting beside him, blushing.

The waitress brought their soup, but he knew even that interruption wouldn't stop the seed he'd just planted. He wanted to bring her pleasure, and he wanted her to be thinking about that, however long it took them to reach that place in their relationship.

"Looks good," he said. Redirecting their focus to the food. "I'm hungry."

She seemed to take a minute to collect herself.

He smiled knowing why she was distracted as he watched her take up the spoon and say in that soft voice, "Yes, it does. I'm hungry, too."

He knew she was hungry for more than her soup. Watching her take a sip, he smiled and reached for his spoon.

They watched each other over their bowls as they took their first spoonfuls their gazes meeting in that intimate getting to know each other way.

He took in the way her lips closed over the spoon and the enjoyment on her face as she ate her soup. Watching her made him wonder how she would look when receiving more intimate pleasures.

ONE BOWL of soup was enough for two people, so they could have shared one since they'd ordered the same thing.

Betsy wished she'd thought of that sooner.

But this was a first date, and maybe he wasn't the kind of guy who liked sharing a meal.

Though he had suggested they share the egg rolls. Maybe if they came here again, she'd suggest that. If he asked her out again that is. If nothing went wrong to stop that.

Look how long it has taken to get this first date off the ground? Maybe we aren't fated to be together despite the attraction between us.

"Must be good. You got quiet," he said.

"Yes, it is very good." She smiled. "And you got quiet too."

"I think we were both pretty hungry when we came in here."

"My stomach was holding a symphony. I'm surprised you didn't hear it in the Jeep on the way here."

"I did, I just didn't mention it."

"Gentlemanly of you."

"I try."

"You succeeded."

"Would you like to go for a drive after dinner over to the river? See the M bridge all lit up?"

"Yes, that would be nice. Then I want to see where you live. And you can show me your bike."

Maybe that wasn't so subtle, but it would let him know she wanted to go to his place afterwards. Not just to see his bike, but for more kissing and for what he had whispered in her ear. She'd been watching his mouth ever since while he ate, covertly, so he wouldn't notice. She couldn't wait to feel his tongue on her skin.

"We can do that." He grinned. "I'd love to show you my place."

"Good." She toyed with her spoon for a moment. "Can I ask you something?"

"Anything you'd like, sweetheart. Ask away."

"About your PTSD. I don't really know how to ask this. How does it...?" she stopped herself, shook her head and started again as he waited patiently for her to finish. "I mean do you take meds? What does it... do? I want to understand."

"You want to know if it's safe to go to my place. If I will flip out or something."

"Well, sort of. But I also want to know how you are, how things are for you."

He let out a breath and leaned back. "Okay. First, don't apologize for wanting to be safe. Never apologize for that. I want you safe too."

"Okay, thank you."

He nodded. "I get flashbacks sometimes. Things trigger it. Sounds. Fireworks. A car backfiring. I don't like large crowds. Sometimes I have bad dreams. But I would never hurt you. Just don't come up to me when I'm asleep and shake me." He gave a great sigh. "As far as meds, the VA doesn't know their ass from a hole in the ground, so they are constantly switching the meds. But I am not on anything heavy duty, and I want to stress again that you are safe with me. The worst I will do is growl at you, and I've already done that."

"Yes, you did, the first day I met you. You were terribly growly that day, and I was a little bit afraid of you."

"I shouldn't have growled at you and this is no excuse, but I was fighting a bad headache that day."

She nodded. "I understand. Are you still getting headaches? Do you get them often?"

"Not as bad as I once did since they adjusted my meds, and I stopped taking one that was making them worse."

"Oh, good. I am glad."

"I'll tell you anything you want to know, and I want you to feel safe with me, but I'd rather talk about happier things right now, if you don't mind."

"Oh, of course I don't mind."

"Your turn. Tell me how you became a librarian, and what you like best about it. It's clear you love your job."

"I've always loved books. Had my nose in one or another since I learned to read. But I wasn't sure what I wanted to be when I went to college. I started off as a history major, but I spent so much time at the library, looking through the stacks and just fascinated by all the treasures in a large college library that finally one of the librarians there befriended me and suggested I go into library science. So I changed majors, and now here I am."

"I'm a history buff too. Primarily military history, but I'm also interested in European renaissance and middle ages."

"Oh, we have that in common too." Betsy laughed. "I used to drive my family nuts. We'd be visiting a historical site and instead of hurrying through the museum I would be reading every single sign and asking questions of the employees and volunteers. I was constantly hearing, "Come on, Betsy, stop poking around." They used to drive me nuts too because I wouldn't always get to read everything on the signs with everyone in such a hurry to get to the next thing."

"I'd never make you hurry. I'd be right alongside of you, reading with you."

"That would be nice. You'd be the first." She smiled.

"Do you like to travel?"

"I do, but it's been a while since I did. How about you?"

"I've seen more of the world than most Americans, but now I'm looking forward to seeing it as a tourist, not as a soldier. Going where I want to go. I like being on the road, driving, going new places and seeing new things. One reason I wanted the Harley."

"I hope you get to travel as much as you'd like to."

"It would be more fun to have a travel companion.'

"I wonder though about you not being there as a soldier." She smiled. "Is it true what they say? Once a Marine always a Marine?"

"Yes. There's no such thing as an ex-Marine. We don't use that term. We are Marine veterans."

"The guys you were out with the other night, were they all Marines too? Did they serve with you?"

"Yes and yes. In one way or another, we served together, and that's how we met."

"I'd like to meet them."

"One of these days when we go out for a beer, I'll invite you along."

"Are there any subjects you don't want to talk about? Things you'd rather I not ask about?"

He was silent for a very long moment and then he said, "No, but understand there are days when I don't want to talk about some things. Days when things happened, and I am remembering friends who have fallen, and days when I just want to forget."

"You're very honest and open."

"I try to be with you. That's the kind of relationship I want, and I'd hope that you would be honest and open with me too."

"I will, Nash. I promise I will," she spoke in that quiet voice with conviction, and her hand reached for his.

His larger, warm, strong fingers wrapped around her smaller soft hand, holding it.

They sat like that for a moment as if honoring the quiet promises they'd made to each other. A good start to the relationship for both of them.

"So," she took a breath and began again. "To lighten things up." She sent him a smile, "What kinds of things do you do for fun when you're not in class?"

"For fun? Beyond training required for my job, I used to play football, ride dirt bikes, lift and go to the rifle range. Haven't done any of that since I got back except for lifting and going to the gun range. I go to the gym every morning and work out. Unless I have a VA appointment to go to. And I work on the bike."

"Very active."

"Yes, very. More so before the accident."

"You like to be outdoors."

"I prefer it."

"I should get out more. More than to work in my flower gardens."

"It's good for you. Fresh air, exercise and a good way to get your thoughts clear."

She brightened. "I like picnics. But it's been a long time since I went on one."

"Then we must go on one once the weather changes. And when the Harley is ready and I've driven her a few times, we can ride it."

"I'd like that. Once the weather changes." Betsy paused, not sure how to ask the question, but she needed to know before she rode on the back of his Harley. "Please forgive me for asking this, but are you going to be able to drive the Harley safely with you missing one eye?"

He was quiet for a minute, and she thought she might have offended him, but then he spoke.

"I've ridden motorcycles of one kind or another since I was fifteen. It won't be as easy to ride as before, but I will make sure it's safe before I ever invite you to ride with me. Your safety comes first, always. Keep in mind I'm driving the Jeep and have to keep just as close an eye on the road driving it. And I know bikes. But I want you to be safe and to feel safe when you are with me."

She didn't know what to say now, and felt a little bit sheepish about it. "I do feel safe when I am with you."

He nodded. "Good."

She took another bite and then pushed her bowl aside. "This was delicious, but I am full."

"It was," he agreed. "I'll stop too before I get too full. We'll both have a good lunch tomorrow."

"Yes, we will." She smiled. "Thank you for dinner. It was delicious."

The waitress came by with the check and two fortune cookies. Nash asked her for two to-go boxes and she went to get them.

"Ready to open your fortune cookie?" He held the tray out to her after removing the bill.

"Yes." She picked the one closest to her. "You open first."

"Okay." He broke the cookie in two and pulled the white slip of paper out. "The short man bears messages."

Well she was not going to ask him to play that game where you read the fortune and say between the sheets. With that fortune it would just have sounded weird.

"Are you expecting any short men?"

"Nope." He shook his head. "Don't know of any."

"Your buddies are all pretty tall like you."

"Yeah, they are. Now open yours."

She broke her cookie and pulled out her fortune. "Worry only causes wrinkles."

"There you go. That's a good one." He nodded. "No worrying for you."

She laughed. "Yes, we wouldn't want me to get all wrinkly or anything."

"You'd be beautiful even with wrinkles, but why bring them on before you have to?"

She blushed at his compliment and smiled. Then her phone went off and she picked it up.

He watched her, thinking how lovely she was when she blushed.

She hit the answer call button and put the phone to her ear. "Hello, Leann. We are still at dinner." Her voice held surprise that her sister was calling, interrupting their date. "What's wrong?" Her eyes grew wide. "Oh, my God. Hang on. Let me tell Nash."

Whatever it was, it had changed her from a beautiful, blushing woman to a woman who was afraid and pale in seconds.

This shit had to stop.

All this drama with her sister who obviously couldn't even give her "favorite sis" a night out free from the drama she brought into her life. Seeing Betsy visually change right in front of him made him want to take the phone and give Leann a good chewing out.

She pulled the phone away from her mouth, looked at Nash and said, "Oh my God, Nash." Her words came fast, falling out of her mouth. "Leann thinks Malcolm has followed her here, to Bartlett. She thought she saw him in the frozen food aisle when she was inside Kroger just minutes ago, and now she's afraid to go back to the house by herself."

Concerned for her sister, his earlier thoughts fled. He reached out his hand for Betsy to hand him the phone. "Let me talk to her."

Betsy handed her phone over.

He put it to his ear. "Where are you now?"

Leann's voice, high pitched and scared came through the phone. "I'm in the car. With the doors locked. But I'm afraid to go home. What if he follows me?"

He listened and then said. "No, don't sit alone in the car. Get out, lock the doors and go back into the grocery. I don't want you sitting in a parking lot by yourself. That's not safe. Go now, while I'm on the phone with you."

CHAPTER EIGHT

*N*ash waited until Leann told him she was inside, and then he said, "We'll be there as soon as we can. Hang tight."

He handed the phone to Betsy. Leaving money on the table and telling their waitress not to worry about the change, he helped Betsy on with her coat and said, "Let's go."

Still courteous as he held doors for her and helped her into the Jeep, this time his attention and his demeanor was on Leann and the problem she might be facing.

Scared for her sister, Betsy appreciated the matter of fact, take charge way he simply took over. His military training snapping into place, a side of him that was a part of him and every other Marine. She knew then what he said was true; there was no such thing as an ex-Marine.

To her, being a Marine meant hero, but to him it was natural, and something he just did. It was his job.

None of the boyfriends she had ever had possessed the qualities and the training that Nash had. Eye patch or not, every man she saw, or had ever seen, paled in comparison to him. Once again, he was charging to the rescue.

She hoped they would reach her sister before something horrible or crazy happened. "I can't believe that nut job has followed her all the way to Bartlett. First her cat, and now this. I hope they catch him and put him away."

Nash set his jaw. "Either way, this asshole won't be bothering her again." He glanced at her. "With your permission, I'll make sure of that."

Not wanting to know what he might do to the man, and wanting nothing more than for her sister to be safe and never bothered by the creep again, she nodded yes.

"Good. We'll be there soon. She's safe inside now. Try not to worry."

"I'll try."

He must've been breaking every speed limit to get them there, so fast, and he was lucky not to have gotten a ticket, but soon they were pulling into the Kroger parking lot where he found a spot and parked the Jeep.

They found Leann inside standing near the

entrance of the store by the stand with the Kroger ads, watching for them.

Betsy hurried up to her and wrapped her in a sisterly hug and then pulled back and said, "I am so glad you are okay."

"I'm glad you're here." Leann's lip quivered and she looked up at Nash. "I didn't know what to do."

"You did fine," he said. "Have you told store security about this? Told anyone here?"

"No," she shook her head. "I didn't think of that."

"I want to talk to the store manager and security,: he said. "Do either of you have his pic with you?"

"Yeah, I've got one in my purse," Leann said. "Campus security suggested I keep it with me for a while, in case I needed to show it to someone."

"Good." Nash nodded. "Come on." He headed toward the store office.

Hours later, after looking through video from the security system and showing the pic to everyone in the store, they reached a dead end.

No one had seen her stalker, and he didn't show up on any of the security cameras.

Nash thanked the store manager and the security people for their time and then said, "Sorry to have put you through all this trouble." Turning he said, "Come on, ladies."

They both followed him out.

Leann said, "I am so sorry. I thought I saw him."

Nash remained silent.

Betsy said, "It's okay, Leann. You just got scared. It will be okay. Let's just get home."

Outside, Leann said to Betsy, "Are you going to ride with me? Since we have two cars here now, Nash won't have to drop you off then."

Nash broke his silence and said, "I'm going there anyway to check out your house and make sure it's safe."

"Oh." Leann then went silent, his tone telling her there was no argument and that he was not a happy man.

"Are you afraid to drive home by yourself?" Betsy asked, ready to ride with her sister.

Nash turned to her. "Why would she be afraid to drive? We'll be right behind her."

Betsy went silent too, and then they were all silent and getting into their cars.

Nash helped her into the Jeep again, closed the door and went around to his side. Getting in, he started the Jeep and waited for Leann to pull out, then pulled out and followed her.

Betsy spoke. "She's just scared, Nash."

"And you're encouraging it."

"What do you mean?"

"There's no reason she couldn't drive herself home, and if you let her wallow in her fears, they will grow bigger. There's already a problem here."

"What problem?"

"She's imagining him behind corners when he's

not there. The guy is probably still on campus with her kitten, miles away from her. If she starts reporting that she's seen him and pulls this with the police, they'll stop listening to her, and you don't want that. Because if he does show up, then she needs to be taken seriously."

"I don't understand why you're upset. She's my baby sister."

"Okay, then." Nash didn't say another word, simply drove behind Leann until they reached Betsy's house. He parked behind Leann's car and then helped Betsy out.

Leann was getting out of her car and looking at them. There would be no privacy between Betsy and Nash, and it was apparent that their date was over.

Ruined by another of Leann's dramas.

Nash was pissed. She'd caused a lot of commotion tonight and for nothing. He wondered how often she pulled this shit, and if her sister was always taken in by it. But what could he do? As Betsy said, Leann was her baby sister. He'd best stay out of it.

"Stay here," he said to the women after unlocking the front door. He went through the house, checking the rooms, the windows and doors to make sure they were locked. Then he came back out and said, "All clear."

The ladies went inside, and he stepped back out. Pausing at the doorway, waiting to see what Betsy would do, he waited for her to turn to him.

When she did, she gave him a sad smile. "Thank you for dinner. It was a nice first date."

"Yes, it was." Key word being was, and maybe he'd emphasized that word a little bit because her eyes widened and then dropped again back into the sadness.

Yes it was. Too bad Leann had ruined it. So much for kisses and a slow tender getting to know each other. We didn't stand a chance as long as her sister keeps pulling her attention away because of neediness and drama.

"All right," he said. "Well, lock up behind me."

"Yes, I will." She gazed up at him.

He wasn't sure what she was thinking or what she wanted. Likely, she was waiting for him to go so she could comfort her sister. "Good night, Betsy."

"Good night, Nash."

WHEN NASH TURNED and walked away, the feeling of sadness that came over Betsy could have knocked her over, it came on so sudden from somewhere deep inside her. She stood watching him get into the Jeep, and then she closed and locked the door as she'd promised.

She stood still with her hand on the door, wishing he'd come back, willing him to come back, and it wasn't until Leann's voice said, "I'm sorry,

Betsy. I really thought I saw him in the store" that she let her hand drop from the door.

Like she'd told Leann before, sorry was a sorry word. She was sick to death of hearing it from her sister. She turned with a bone deep sigh and went over to the couch where her sister sat curled with her arms around her legs in that little girl pose she always took. She looked at Leann, and suddenly she was too tired to deal with her sister and her problems. She was tired down to her bones with the whole thing.

Leann talked about her stalker every single day.

Betsy hadn't had a break from it. Until tonight. Until that lovely date with Nash tonight. Which Leann had yet to ask about. Which Leann had yet to apologize for interrupting. She and Nash hadn't even had a good night kiss. It was all too much, and now she wanted to be done with the whole evening.

Tonight Betsy was too tired to sit and deal with her sister and all her worries, her problems. "I'm going to bed, Leann. We're locked in. Get some sleep. I'll see you in the morning."

Leann's jaw dropped open.

Betsy turned and went down the hall. She couldn't wait to get out of these shoes and this dress.

So much for feeling sexy and looking sexy. Might as well have worn jeans and a t-shirt.

"Good night, sis," Leann called to her.

Betsy heard her, but didn't respond. She didn't have anything else to say tonight.

In her room, she stepped out of the red shoes and peeled out of the red dress. She sat at her dressing table in front of the mirror and wiped off her makeup using the makeup remover cloths she kept there for that. The sight of her red lipstick made her want to cry.

He'd not had a chance to remove hardly any of it. She was sadder than she had been in a very long time.

One tear rolled down her cheek and then another. She put her face in her hands and let the tears flow silently so her sister wouldn't hear. After she cried for a while she slowly got up and peeled out of her underwear. Then she grabbed her oldest, softest big t-shirt that she liked to sleep in and crawled into bed. She wrapped the covers around herself and curled into a ball, wanting nothing but comfort around her and sleep.

Leann knocked on the door.

Betsy didn't answer.

"Betsy? Are you still awake?"

Betsy remained silent wishing her sister would go away and leave her in peace for the night.

The door cracked open and light came into the room just as her sister poked her head through. "Bets? Hey, I know you're upset. And I'm guessing you're not asleep." She stepped into the room leaving the door open as more light spilled in. "I can't sleep either. So can we talk?"

Betsy rolled onto her back and stared up at the ceiling with a sigh.

Her sister was not respecting the closed door and once again focused all on herself.

"I don't know why you are so upset with me." Leann stepped closer. "Oh hey, have you been crying? What's wrong, sis? Did Nash do something mean to you?"

"No. Nash has been perfect. The evening would have been perfect."

"Until I ruined it." Leann's tone showed she was finally catching on.

"You said it, I didn't," Betsy said.

"But it's what you were thinking and anyway, it's the truth. I'm sorry, sis. Maybe I should just go back to campus and stop ruining your life."

Betsy sat up. "No, don't do that. You are not ruining my life."

"I came here to visit and brought trouble with me."

Well Betsy wasn't about to argue with that. "I'm still glad you came to visit. But you've got to stop freaking out about Malcolm. He's got you so spooked you're seeing him behind every corner. And it's got to stop."

"I know, sis. I'll try to stop freaking out. It's hard though."

Leann went over and picked up Betsy's red dress and looked at it as if she'd never seen it before. "You like Nash a lot, don't you? More than you let on."

"Yes, I do." Betsy nodded.

"He'll call you again, sis." Leann hung the dress on a hanger. "I can tell he's really into you too."

"I hope so."

"He'll call. I'd bet money on it."

Betsy hoped Leann was right.

"Forgive me?"

Betsy sighed. "Yes, I forgive you."

Leann came over and gave her a hug. "Thanks, sis."

Now close the door and let me get some sleep."

"Okay. Good night." Leann left, closing the door softly.

AFTER DROPPING Betsy off Nash headed home with the local rock station cranked as high as he could stand it. Pissed at the situation, he knew he wouldn't get to sleep for a long time tonight.

He pulled into his garage, parked the car and put the garage door down, but didn't bother going into the house. Shrugging out of his jacket, he tossed it on the hood of the car and went over to where a punching bag hung in the back of the garage.

Flexing his hands, he reached for the tape and began to wrap them.

He'd work the stress and frustration out tonight with as many punches as it took to make him get over the possibility of losing his dream girl and the anger at Malcolm Hess who he'd really like to punch out.

It took quite a few rounds to wear himself out. When he was done, he went into the kitchen, grabbed a beer and went back to work on the Harley.

After an hour and another beer, he was frustrated with the bike. He'd run into a troublesome spot repairing it. Finally, he picked up the phone and called his buddy James.

"Hey, Jim, you busy?"

"No, bro, what's up?"

"I hit a rough patch putting this bike back together."

"Thought you were out with the librarian tonight?"

"Yeah, that didn't go as planned."

"How about I swing by and take a look at the bike. My exciting evening is doing laundry. It can wait."

"Thanks. I've got a beer here with your name on it."

"Headed out the door in five."

Once Jim arrived they cracked open a couple of beers and started working together on the bike.

"Your date ended earlier than you'd planned." Jim took a sip of beer and then set the bottle down to free his hands again to work on the bike. "Everything okay with you and Betsy?"

"Yes, it was until her sister freaked out in the grocery store."

"Leann?" Jim's eyes showed how interested he was in Betsy's sister. "What was she freaking out about?"

"She thought a guy who'd been following her around on campus had showed up down here and was following her again at the grocery store. She called from the parking lot freaking out so Betsy and I went straight there from the restaurant. The guy didn't show up on any of the security tapes. It was a false alarm."

"Damn. Glad it was a false alarm. But that sucks it ruined your date."

"She's a drama queen."

"Who, Betsy?"

"No. Leann."

"Aw she's just high strung." Jim laughed. "You just gotta know how to handle a girl like that."

"Not my type, bro." Nash shook his head. "I had enough of that with my ex- fiancé. That kind of woman creates drama where there isn't any because they can't live without it. Leann is all yours."

"I'll gladly take her on." Jim grinned. "She's a hottie. How long is she visiting? I'd like to ask her out."

"She may be moving here to go to the University of Memphis. She's been looking into transferring."

"Good. Now about her sister. How did you leave things?"

Nash shrugged. "Just said good night."

"That's it?"

"Well yeah."

"Aw, bro. You got to leave them with something to keep them thinking about you. If not a kiss, then something, maybe plans for the next date. You can't just say good night. That ends everything on a down note."

"Yep. It was already on a down note."

Jim reached for Nash's cell phone and held it out to him. "Text her now with either a sweet nothing or tell her you can't wait to see her again and then ask her out on a second date."

Nash took the phone and looked at it. "It's kinda late."

"If she likes you, she won't mind the lateness. Go on. Send it."

Nash pulled up her number and sent a message.

Beautiful lady in red, I enjoyed our dinner. Would like to see you again. Movie or dancing, your choice. Next weekend?

He hit send and then looked back at Jim. "There. Done."

"If she's awake, you'll hear back right away."

Nash watched his phone for a few minutes, hoping to hear from her, but nothing came through.

"You been having any more of those headaches?"

"Not since they changed my meds. I'm hoping they are gone."

"Me too."

Nash then put the cell phone back on the table. "She's probably asleep by now."

"Yeah, it's getting late. I ought to be going. Let me know how it turns out with Betsy." He stood and pulled on his jacket and then paused. "This guy who was following Leann around. If he keeps harassing her, you and me could go pay him a visit. Make him see the error of his ways."

"Thanks, bro. If it needs doing, I'll let you know."

Jim nodded and then looked at the bike. "She's coming along. If you need any more help, give me a call."

Nash nodded. "Thanks for coming over."

"You're welcome."

$\mathcal{A}$nother week passed.

Betsy never answered his text. But then she called around eight on Friday night when Nash was at the pub having a beer with his buddies,

"Nash, Leann thinks she saw Malcolm. Help. I don't know what to do. I think I saw him too."

"I'm at Celtic Crossing. Where are you?"

"WolfChase Mall."

"Find a security guard and tell him. I'm on my way."

"We will as soon as she comes out of the ladies room."

"You're in a store restroom I hope."

"No, it's the main one by the carousel."

Damn it. That wasn't good. More women are robbed and raped in those restrooms than any other place in a mall.

He didn't want her to panic any more than she already was so he only said, "Get out of there."

"She's still in the stall. I'm waiting."

"Tell her to hurry. Just get out and find security. Now. I'm on my way. Keep your phone on.

He threw on his jacket. "Gotta go guys. Catch you later." Then he grabbed his keys and headed out the door.

I'm going to make sure the girls are safe, and then I hope he does show his face. I'll kick his ass.

In the car he dialed Betsy again. When she answered he said, "Where are you now?"

"Still in the ladies room."

"I thought you were leaving, following my directions."

"We are, I promise."

"Okay, stay on the line talking to me. I'm driving that way now. Where did you see him?"

"Leann saw him on the other side of the mall, walking along parallel to us, but when I looked and saw him, he ducked into a store."

"And you're sure it was him."

"Yes, I saw him too and it was a bath and soaps kind of store he went into. Kind of girly for a guy to be going into when it's not Christmas or Valentine's Day. Leann thought so too and we both think he's been following us."

"Betsy, are you sure it was him?"

"I'd bet money on it."

"Okay, you need to get out of there. Head toward the entrance of the mall where there are people. Keep talking to me. I'm on my way. I'll be there in twenty minutes."

Betsy knocked on the restroom stall and yelled at Leann, "Hurry up, we have to get out of here."

"Oh my God, is he here?" Leann flushed and then the door opened and she rushed out still buttoning her jeans.

"No time to talk, just come on. We need to go now." Betsy took her by the arm with one hand, the other still holding packages, both hers and Leann's.

They hurried through the mall and made almost to the entrance before Betsy's phone died. She put it to her ear to talk to Nash and then realizing it had gone dead, said, "Oh no."

"What's wrong?" Leann grabbed her arm, eyes wide with fear.

"My phone is dead. Come on, we'll get to the car and I'll put it on charge and call Nash back."

They went out past the entrance into the parking lot heading for Betsy's car.

As they got near the car, a white van parked beside it turned on and then a door slid open and a man stepped out.

"Malcolm," Leann gasped.

Malcolm was short and compact in his twenties, and he obviously lifted because his arms were so big.

Brown, average hair and wire rimmed glasses made him look smart and studious, but Betsy could only see him as a monster, one that was after her sister.

"Leann." He pointed to a cage on the seat. "Get in. Mr. Whiskers wants you."

"Oh, my God. My Whiskers," Leann dropped her packages and moved toward the open van door.

Betsy grabbed her by the arm and pulled her back. "No, Leann. Don't."

"Give him to me," Leann said holding her arms out for the kitten.

"No. You're coming back home with me where you belong."

"Listen you crazy man. My sister isn't going anywhere with you," Betsy yelled.

"If she wants Mr. Whiskers she is. And if she doesn't," he pulled out a knife and waved it in the air making Leann shriek. "Goodbye, Mr. Whiskers."

Malcolm lunged at them with the knife, and both women screamed.

Betsy automatically took a step back when he lunged, but Leann had frozen like a doe in headlights.

Malcolm had grabbed her. "You're coming with me now," he said.

"No," Leann screamed and struggled to get away.

"Let her go," Betsy reached for her sister again, stepping forward.

But Malcolm had the knife and her sister and he pulled Leann backward toward the open van door.

Nash's Jeep pulled up nearby, squealing tires as he pulled into the space next to them in a diagonal, not bothering with parking lines or rules.

He leapt out, leaving the door open and the Jeep running.

Malcolm, distracted by Nash's sudden arrival, took his attention off Leann just long enough for her to stomp on his foot as she bent down, and then raising up she slammed her head back trying to hit his chin and being too short, missed it and hit his chest.

Nash moved in with controlled fury as Leann dropped. Grabbing Malcolm's knife arm, he twisted it.

The knife dropped, clattering on the concrete.

Leann stood again, looking dazed, perhaps dizzy from her attempted head butt.

Nash pulled her around behind him, saying, "Get back."

She moved to his instructions, and Betsy wrapped her arm around her, "Come on, sis," moving her back further from the men.

Seeing Leann free enraged Malcolm. He charged Nash.

Nash threw a punch hitting Malcolm on the jaw, dazing him.

But then Malcom came at Nash again.

Nash punched him in the ribs.

Malcolm bent over, his breath gone momentarily, but then he was back and even angrier.

Betsy watched in horror.

My God. The man just keeps coming. Will he never stop? Will Nash be able to stop him? Malcolm is crazy. His eyes say it, and he keeps on coming even through Nash's punishing blows where a normal man would have stopped.

She prayed Nash would not be hurt. He appeared to be winning the fight, but with a crazy man like Malcolm who might do anything, Betsy still worried.

Leann, perhaps sensing her worry, or needing comfort herself, wrapped her arms around Betsy. They stood holding onto each other.

Nash moved behind Malcolm, wrapping one arm around his neck and using the other to lock that hold and squeeze tight. His expression fierce and strong, he squeezed.

This time, when Nash grabbed hold of the bad guy with that murderous look in his eyes, Betsy wasn't afraid. All her worry that Nash would be hurt fled. She was glad he was the kind of man who could take a bad guy down and had what it took to do it.

Malcolm couldn't get air and went limp.

Betsy didn't think he was getting up again, and if he tried, Nash wasn't going to let him.

~

NASH SAW the scene unfolding like a bad movie as he pulled into the parking lot.

Malcolm was moving to grab Leann, and he had a knife.

Nash leapt out of his Jeep, keys still in it, running.

His mind moved fast assessing.

Weapon. Knife.

Control the knife. Disarm.

The three ways he could do that.

Evaluate. Choose. Move. Now.

Everything outside of the threat faded to the periphery as he closed in with narrowed focus, his training and instincts kicked into high gear.

He grabbed Malcolm's wrist and twisted.

The knife fell to the ground.

Nash punched Malcolm's face. Within seconds, the girl was freed. But she stood frozen, stunned.

Move.

"Get back," he commanded as he moved her behind him, taking charge.

The girl safely behind him, he moved in now, angry. This fight was now personal, and he wanted to do some damage.

He could have left it to the cops and the court. The girls were safe now. But if he left it, this would happen again, and it would keep happening until

Malcolm had the girl or she was dead. He might even come after Betsy to get to Leann.

And that was not happening.

This ended now.

Malcolm lunged at Nash with a roar of rage.

Nash locked both hands around the back of Malcolm's neck and rammed his knee into Malcolm's torso.

Malcolm tried to return punches to Nash's ribs but failed to get enough power.

Nash reared back and slugged Malcolm across the face. The punch dazed Malcolm, and he stumbled back. But he kept on coming.

Malcolm threw a haymaker swing and Nash dodged it.

Nash's right hand shot up in reflex driven by a twist of his hips and torso into Malcolm's ribs. He felt bones crack beneath his hand.

Malcolm crumpled, his breath gone momentarily, but then he straightened again, wincing and angry.

Then Nash grabbed Malcolm, and wrapping his arms around Malcolm's neck, put him in a sleeperhold, squeezing, cutting off blood flow to Malcolm's brain.

Malcolm went limp.

Nash kept on squeezing.

Just a few more minutes, and it would be done.

From his training, he knew within minutes Malcolm would be dead.

Mall security was now running up to them yelling. "Hands in the air."

He looked up and over at Betsy who stood watching him as she held on to her sister. The fear was gone from her eyes and instead they were filled with relief and gratitude.

Their gazes met and locked.

Nash could have held on just a minute longer. Just enough to take Malcolm out for good.

Without a weapon, Nash was on the defensive and there were witnesses that had seen Malcolm with the knife. Shoppers stood watching.

He was justified in taking the man out. Leann would never have to worry about this man again and neither would any other girl.

A few more seconds, and it would be over.

But he looked into Betsy's eyes. Her eyes shone with emotion telling him that right now she was seeing him as her hero.

Just a few more seconds.

Still her gaze held him, unwavering, seeing him as that hero.

No.

And then he let go, raising his arms into the air, Malcolm's body dropping to the ground.

"Call an ambulance," he told the security guard

as he kept his hands in the air. "And the police. This asswipe tried to abduct a girl."

He'd ask for the police. Show he had nothing to hide.

The demeanor of the security guard changed as an older security guard joined him and said, "I already called it in. I'll call for an ambulance."

Sirens and blue lights blazing, a police car pulled into the parking lot.

Malcolm lay on the ground.

Nash stood with his hands in the air.

The policemen quickly took over from the security guards who seemed relieved.

One policeman quickly patted Nash down, and seeing he had no weapons, let him put his hands down.

"What happened here?" the policeman said.

"That man tried to abduct my sister! With a knife!" Betsy said, her voice high and excited with emotion as she pointed. "And this man saved her."

An ambulance pulled up and two EMT's jumped out and rushed to put Malcolm on a stretcher, working on him in a hurry while the policemen continued to question Nash, Betsy, and Leann.

"He's got broken ribs," one EMT said.

"And a punctured lung," the other said.

Nash listened, knowing the man would probably die anyway from his injuries. There'd been no need to finish him off with Betsy watching. She didn't need to see that. That, too, he would protect her from. He never wanted to see that light in her eyes fade from something he had done. He just wanted her safe. And far away from the ugliness that men sometimes had to do to protect their women.

Malcolm never made it to the hospital. He died in the parking lot from a collapsed lung.

The police took statements from everyone at the scene who had seen anything.

Leann was united with Mr. Whiskers who had lost so much weight he looked like he hadn't been fed in weeks. She kept cuddling the kitten and whispering to him once she'd stopped crying.

Betsy, though quiet, seemed less shaken by the ordeal and focused on being the support for her sister while being quite vocal with the police about everything Nash had done to save them.

Nash was free to go, Malcolm was dead, and no arrest was made.

"I want to thank you," Betsy said.

"No need to thank me," he said.

"Oh, but there is," she said. "It's not nearly enough. But I want to bring a pizza over to your place. Just a small way of thanking you. If that is okay with you."

"Oh, you do?"

"Yes, I do. If that is okay with you. I'll understand if you don't want me to come over."

"All right." He smiled. "I do like pizza. And why

wouldn't I want you to come over? That's a silly thing to say."

"Good." She smiled in return. "I'm glad it's okay. I just want you to know I'm not expecting anything beyond friendship. I'm not, you know, chasing you or anything. I mean I understand if you don't want to date me any more."

"Whoa, slow down there. What are you talking about?" He shook his head at her in confusion. "You're not making any sense."

"Well after our last date," she paused and looked away from him embarrassment flooding her cheeks.

"I texted you that night. Asked you out again. You never answered."

Her gaze flew to his, her eyes wide. "You did?"

He nodded.

"I never got it." Her words rushed out.

As they both realized what had happened and the air was cleared between them they both relaxed into smiles and their gazes danced together.

He raised one eyebrow. "So, pizza. My place. Tomorrow night."

Her smile was as wide as the sky as she giggled. "Yes sir."

Betsy showed up at his front door the next night with a large pizza and that same big smile.

"Well, hello," he said, opening the door. "Come on in."

She entered carrying the pizza box and said, "Where should I put the pizza?"

He said, "I'll take it" and reached out for the box.

She handed the box to him and then followed him into the kitchen. But she stopped short just inside the doorway, seeing the Harley engine on his kitchen table.

He placed the pizza box on the stove, and then noting her reaction said, "We don't have to eat in here."

"Oh, no, I'm fine with anywhere. Anywhere you like."

"I have paper plates and napkins." He got them out of the cabinet and placed them beside the pizza box. "What would you like to drink? I have beer, grape juice and water."

"I'm good with water. Never been much of a beer drinker."

"Gotcha." He winked and then taking a glass filled it with water and then handed it to her.

"I'm not used to company."

"And I'm not used to showing up with pizza on a man's doorstep."

"Well, I sure am glad you did. Sweetheart, you can show up on my doorstep any time you like."

"I'd like that." She smiled. "I wanted to thank you for saving my sister from that crazy man. God only knows what would have happened to her if Malcolm had gotten her into that van." She shivered.

He stood watching her and listening, his mood changing from playful to quiet as he listened.

"That man was..." she shivered again.

Nash kissed her then, ever so gently, his lips brushing across hers.

All thoughts of Malcolm went away, banished from her thoughts just as he'd made the threat of Malcolm go away.

Now there was only the tenderness of Nash's lips upon hers and the sweetness of every first kiss she had ever had, though this wasn't their first kiss, along with something more, something unnamed and full of promise.

She responded, and he deepened the kiss.

Kissing him was like kissing any other man with her eyes closed, as she always did, and yet this kiss was unlike any other. Sweeter, more tender, more full of promise. A kiss to be swept away in. Yet she wanted to see him, just peeks, instead of being swept away like this. She wanted a visual to remember this moment forever.

She opened her eyes slightly to peek at him and saw how his eye was closed, how he too was swept away in kissing her.

The glimpse of a dreaming boy, and of a carefree and careful man was all there for her to see.

The eye patch didn't matter. It wasn't even

slightly scary to her now up close, this close. She didn't care what the eye patch was covering. Maybe it was a horrible scar.

Whatever it was didn't matter.

He was her hero, her Marine. He'd saved her sister's life. He was one of the good guys, the defenders. Now she understood him better and wondered what she had ever been afraid of.

She kissed him without fear, holding nothing back, closing her eyes again, this time to be swept away in their blissfully shared kiss.

The kiss deepened, tongues tangling, until her breath came heavier, desire now flowing as if a dam had released its floodwaters, and there was nothing left to hold it back. Letting go built her desire for him.

"Nash, please," she breathed the words as they came up for air.

"Please what?" He smiled. "Please stop. Please pizza. Please…"

"Pizza can wait. And no, don't stop. Please." She smiled.

His gaze holding hers, he slipped his hands beneath her sweater and slid them up her belly, moving them warm and slow.

She was growing much too hot and wanted her sweater off. Pulling on the bottom of the sweater, she tried to raise it up.

Then his hands took over, pulling the sweater off and over her head.

She stood in bra and jeans in front of him.

He looked down at her breasts beneath the black lace bra and inhaled a breath. "Beautiful," he said. "I wonder if your panties match."

She opened her mouth to speak, to tell him yes.

But he placed a finger upon her lips and said, "I like discovering you, so let me have the anticipation."

Smiling beneath his finger, she gave a small nod.

He released his finger and followed it with a kiss upon her lips.

She unbuttoned his shirt and eased it off his shoulders to see his broad bare shoulders and a chest that would have been photograph worthy if not for the scattering of scars.

"Shrapnel," he said as he watched her expression.

She bent to kiss one scar.

He inhaled with a hiss before her lips upon his skin soothed him into a long exhale.

The sound was as if he'd been holding something inside for a very long time.

If he would allow her, she would kiss every one of his scars. If she could, she would kiss away everything he held tight inside. She wanted him to feel loved and whole, not like less of a man.

He was more man than most men she knew.

There was nothing wrong with him in her eyes. Even missing one eye, to her, he was perfect.

Now, he moved to remove her jeans, and as he slid them over her hips, he smiled. Now the matching panties were visible. From his expression, he liked what he saw.

She was happy the sight of her pleased him, and what she saw mirrored in his eyes made her feel very beautiful. Stepping out of her jeans, she reached for his belt buckle and fumbled with it a little bit.

He covered her hands with his and said, "Slow down. Enjoy. We have all night."

It was nerves that made her fumble, and she looked up at him and blushed. "I am showing my lack of experience in this area. Most of the guys I have been with just shucked themselves out of their jeans as fast as they could."

"Probably thought if they didn't hurry, you'd change your mind."

"Once I really should have." She laughed. "But I didn't kick him out until the next morning."

"Well, I hope you don't want to kick me out, sweetheart."

"Oh no, I'd never kick you out." She had his jeans past his hips now and was sliding them down his legs. "In fact, I couldn't as this is your place."

"True," he said, stepping out of his jeans. "But you could always kick me into the living room."

She laughed. "I'd never kick you anywhere.

You're my hero, don't you know? I don't want to be kicking you, I want to be kissing you. All night long."

His answer was to sweep her into a deep kiss that made her head spin, before lifting her up into his arms to carry her into his bedroom.

THE END

Bartlett Police Officer Leonard "Len" Yardley was less than thrilled to be on desk duty while his arm and shoulder healed from a gunshot wound he'd received a week ago. But that was the rule of the precinct and doctor's orders. So, Len was stuck inside at a desk filling out paperwork. It hadn't put him in the best of moods.

Civilians had no idea how much paperwork cops did, even the cops out in patrol cars. Paperwork was his least favorite thing about his job. He liked having his feet on the ground, meeting challenges head on and moving forward into them. That was his way. To be out among the people, or driving the streets and keeping them safe. Not stuck inside an office all day.

He was restless, but looking forward to attending a cookout next Saturday at Nash Ware's place. Nash was planning to ask his girlfriend to marry him and if she said yes, the barbecue would be a celebration of their engagement.

Nash's girl, Betsy Bobbin, was a quiet librarian who worked at the Bartlett Library. Nash was clearly head over heels in love with her. True love was good to see. Too often Len saw the other side of people. He needed the reminder that some marriages were good ones and actually meant to last.

****

Len opted to wear a loose Hawaiian print shirt which covered his bandage. No one would know he was hurt unless he told them.

Leaving his Harley in the garage, he drove his truck to Nash's house and parked down the street.

Already the street was lined with cars. Nash's driveway and the drive next door were full, so Len parked one street over. Other than the nine-millimeter Len always carried, along with his spare pistol and his I.D., which wouldn't come out unless it was necessary, nothing marked him as a cop.

He walked toward Nash's house, taking in the other houses and checking Nash's out.

Len had met the Marine veteran with the eye patch at the local Harley dealership fundraiser ride for the children's hospital last month.

Nash had an unusual set up, on account of having sight in only one eye. He had a series of custom mirrors mounted on his bike to give him good visibility and he rode a 2003 Harley Road King, one hundredth anniversary special, that he'd restored after he came home from the Middle East.

He also preferred to ride with at least one other biker, so for the children's fundraising ride, they'd paired up. Len had enjoyed getting to know the quiet Marine vet. He was, as Len's grandfather would have said, "a solid guy." They'd stayed in touch, and Len had been invited to the barbecue.

Walking to the backyard fence, he pushed the door open and looked for Nash. Spotting the Marine over by the barbecue grill, Len stepped out and walked over to him. "Hey, Nash, great day for a barbecue."

"It is," Nash shook his hand and then glanced up at the sky using his good eye to get a good look. He grinned. "Not one rain cloud in sight."

Last week they'd had rain every single day. Sunshine and blue clouds were a welcome sight.

The back door opened and a pretty woman with long blonde hair and blue eyes stepped out carrying an oven mitt. "Betsy sent this out for you and said Pete's running late. He's bringing more ice and a big tub of vanilla ice cream."

Nash grinned. "This party just gets better and better. Leanne, I'd like you to meet Officer Len Yardley."

So much for no one knowing he was a cop. But that didn't matter now.

"Hello," Len said, smiling down at the prettiest girl there. With her beautiful smile, nice curves and a glow which went beyond her lightly tanned skin, she could have stepped out of his dreams. He wanted to get to know her.

"Hello," she said, smiling up at him. "It's nice to meet you, Officer Yardley."

"You can call me Len."

"Len, I'm glad you could come to the celebration," she said. "This is a big day for my sister, Betsy. And for Nash."

She was clearly happy for her sister. She almost bubbled over with genuine excitement. It shone in her eyes and across her face. Rosy cheeks and bright blue eyes looked back at him.

He couldn't help but smile deeper.

"Officer Yardley is with the Bartlett Police Department," Nash said.

"Ooh a policemen," Leann looked up at Len with new admiration. "I love policemen."

Len smiled at her and wondered why she looked familiar. Maybe it was her resemblance to her sister Betsy.

"How long have you been a policeman?"

"I wanted to be a cop ever since I was a little kid, so the minute I graduated from Bartlett High School, I signed up to be a military cop with the Air Force.

Served six years in security forces and made sergeant before coming home to join the Bartlett Police Department. I've been there two years," he said.

"Oh wow. So, are you one of the men who came to the mall after that stalker tried to abduct me?"

His face went serious. "No, I wasn't there. You had a stalker?"

"It's a long story," she shrugged. "I'd bore you."

"This party just started," he said. "We have plenty of time and no, you won't bore me. Tell me."

"This was two years ago. That's why I thought you were one of the policemen who was there."

"I would've been newly hired and likely writing traffic tickets. Everyone starts out that way. So, what happened?"

Leann's sister Betsy, the librarian, came out the back door of the house, carrying a bowl of coleslaw and two big packages of buns. She placed them on the long table just beyond the barbecue grill. "I thought I bought four packages of buns but they weren't in the grocery bags. So, I called Jim. He's picking up two more on his way," she said.

"That's great, honey," Nash said. "And Lance is bringing some kind of vegetarian dish because his new girlfriend doesn't eat meat."

"I'm glad they're bringing something she can eat," she said, her eyes wide. "I didn't think about anyone being vegetarian. All three of your buddies will be late. I guess we'd better let everyone start eating and not wait on them."

"Betsy, stop fussing. Come and meet Len," Leann said.

Betsy walked up to them, and they were introduced.

Len had seen Betsy and knew of the pretty librarian but hadn't met her.

She has a sweet motherly nature. No wonder the children of Bartlett love story hour at the library with Miss Betsy.

"Everything is ready, so dig in," Betsy said, but her soft voice didn't carry enough to be heard.

Nash told everyone, louder, in his Marine voice.

Len grinned. Marines and cops learned how to use a commanding voice people heard immediately. He could see Nash commanding troops.

Party goers lined up and began filling their plates.

Len got in line behind Leann and hoped they'd continue their conversation after they went through the line.

When each had a plate full of food he said, "Where do you want to sit?"

"Over by the bird feeder," she said.

He glanced around the yard but didn't see one.

"The black pedestal with the lamp on top," Leann said.

Then he realized the lamp was a bird feeder open on each side instead of having glass panels.

"Nash likes to tinker with things taking other things out of them," Leann said. "He's very creative."

"Clever idea."

They headed to two seats nearby and sat by a small table. The cozy arrangement might help her share her story.

After they were seated, he said, "You were telling me what happened with your stalker."

"I was in college at Eastern Kentucky and had two more years to finish my degree in marketing. There was a guy in my algebra class who developed a crush on me. He signed up to be my tutor and tried to get close, but he wasn't my type, so I didn't let him."

His eyebrow went up. "Someone in your class signed up to be your tutor?"

"Yeah, that didn't raise a red flag for me at the time," she admitted. "My sister pointed that out later. He seemed to think I was his girlfriend even though I kept turning him down for dates. He was always texting me or messaging me on social media. It was like he watched every single thing I did. I needed to keep going to tutoring because I suck at algebra and I needed to pass."

"You couldn't find another tutor?"

"Well I didn't think of it," she admitted. "Then I

came to Bartlett to visit my sister, Betsy, and he messaged me about my kitten, Mr. Whiskers."

Len smiled at the name and then forced the smile away to be serious again as he listened.

"He kidnapped Mr. Whiskers on campus. But I was afraid to talk to him even though I knew he had Mr. Whiskers. He really creeped me out. A *lot*."

"You had a good reason to be creeped out," Len said. "A pattern of abusing animals is a red flag for criminal behavior. Always trust your gut feeling."

"He turned out to be even crazier. After those texts, he came to Bartlett with my kitten. He wanted me to get into his van to get my fur baby. I wanted to rescue Mr. Whiskers."

"I yelled at her not to do it," Betsy had walked over as they spoke. "We'd just come out of the Wolf-Chase Galleria Mall, and he'd parked his white van right next to my car. He was waiting inside, ready to entice her with her kitten in a cage."

"I just wanted Mr. Whiskers," Leann said. "I didn't know he had a knife."

"Never get in the vehicle. For any reason," Len said. "Do everything you can to stay out of it, scream, shout, fight."

"I wasn't going to get in," she shook her head. "I knew to listen to Betsy. But he had a knife. And he grabbed me."

"I'd called Nash, and he was on his way," Betsy said. "Thank God. It was terrifying."

"When Malcom grabbed me and tried to pull me into the van, Nash pulled up in his truck and went for him. He saved my life."

"Malcom," Len said. "Would that be Malcom Hess?"

"Yes, that's him," Leann nodded.

"I recall hearing about him after they hired me. He had a prior history of stalking. He never made it to trial and died in the hospital."

"They took him away in an ambulance. He had broken ribs and a punctured lung. That killed him before they could save him. I was so glad. He'd terrorized me for months. Now I'll never have to see him again. And I was so glad I had Mr. Whiskers back."

"I'm glad, too. And how is Mr. Whiskers today?"

"He's not a kitten any more, but he's still a noisy night owl, and he gets into everything. He's been very naughty this month. Between finals and graduation, I haven't been home much."

"Graduation?"

"Leann just graduated from the University of Memphis with a BA in marketing," Betsy said, clearly proud of her sister.

"Congratulations," he smiled at Leann.

"Thank you," she said, smiling back.

"What's next?" he asked.

"I start working at Southern Security Bank," she said. "Assistant manager of the Bartlett branch."

"Nice," he said.

"Yes," she nodded. "It's the most adult job I've ever had. Lots of responsibility."

"If they didn't think you were up to it, they wouldn't have hired you."

"True, I suppose." She nodded.

"No supposing. Bankers are dry and careful people," he said. "They're careful not to make mistakes."

"I wore my sisters most conservative suit to the interview," she said. "I think that helped."

"I'm sure it did," he said.

"Two years ago, Leanne was in her sorority party girl phase," Betsy said. "Picture bleach blonde hair, black leather skirt and black leather boots."

"Nothing wrong with leather," Len said. He didn't mention his Harley. Today he'd driven the truck.

Leann in leather. She'd be hot.

"Your natural color looks better than that white blonde," Betsy said to Leann. "It goes with your skin tone. I'm sure the conservative look helped you get the bank job."

"I think so too." Leann nodded. "They even have a dress code! I didn't know anyone still did that!"

"A college campus isn't the real world," Betsy said. "I can't imagine going to class in pajamas. I don't even run to the drugstore for a prescription dressed like that when I'm sick."

Leann laughed. "No, you wouldn't. I've been to classes at EKU and to get ice cream in mine."

"Ice cream?" Betsy's eyes widened, and she shook her head.

Len quietly laughed. The two sisters were very different. He wasn't about to tell them he didn't own a pair of pajamas. He threw on exercise shorts and carried his gun if he went to answer his front door. Most nights he slept commando.

"Back then I never worried about anything, least of all what someone thought about what I was wearing. These days I'm looking for more security in my life." Leann had turned serious. "Hey, speaking of security, when is the big announcement?"

"Right after everyone eats their barbecue and before the cake comes out. We even have an engagement cake!" Betsy said.

"If it's supposed to be a secret, you're not keeping it very well." Leann laughed. "You might want to whisper."

"Whispering makes people listen closer, and a whisper can carry," Len dropped his voice low. "For a secret, it's better to lower your voice, like this."

LEANN, leaning in to hear him better, breathed in, catching his scent.

His cologne is nice. His smile is even nicer. And his muscles? The nicest of all.

She didn't mind getting closer to him. Being near him raised her senses to a level she hadn't reached with anyone. Even the colors around them seemed brighter. It had to be pheromones, and his sexy voice did a number on her inside.

I wish he'd talk to me more in that low, sexy voice.

"I wonder what kind of cake it is," she murmured, her voice now low too.

"Carrot cake with cream cheese icing," Betsy said. "I went with Nash's favorite. But he doesn't know."

"Sounds delicious," Len said.

"What's your favorite cake?" Leann asked Len.

"Red Velvet," he said.

"Oh, that's a good one," Leann said. "I've never made one of those. Just strawberry or chocolate. Betsy is the baker."

"Do you cook?" he asked Leann.

"Oh yeah. That's my chili dip over there. I've got a big pot of chili at home. Always make a lot when I take my chili dip somewhere. I end up freezing it because it's more than Betsy and I can eat."

"I'll have to try your dip," he said. "Sounds good." He made a point of getting up to go help himself to her dip and corn chips to dip into it.

Betsy watched him go. "Kind of old for you, isn't he?"

Leann frowned. "No. And anyway, we're just talking."

"Right. That's why you're leaning in, showing off your cleavage. Just take it slow, please, and be careful."

"Betsy, he's a *cop*. You don't find a safer guy to date than a cop. And if he's older, so what? I *like* him. And besides he hasn't asked me out. We just met."

"Oh, he's interested. Please go slow. You just broke up with Stanford."

"Yeah, well, Stanford is an ass. A wealthy one, but still an ass. Officer Yardley is nothing like Stanford."

Stanford Westland the third. God's gift to women. Or so he thinks. He has impeccable manners, high standards, and he was charming at first. God only knows what makes him criticize everything about me now, when he supposedly liked me so much in the beginning.

Len came back with food on his plate and a large helping of her dip. He sat down. "Your dip is good. I snuck a bite."

"Testing it before you loaded up?" she laughed. "Making sure I wouldn't poison you."

He laughed. "No poisoning allowed. My coworkers would be all over you."

"I guess that's true!" she laughed.

Oh good. Not only is he a sexy cop, he has a good sense of humor, too.

"I'm glad you like my dip," she said. "My ex-boyfriend has been telling me for months I don't make it right. Apparently, I don't cook anything right."

"He's an idiot," Len said, "Look at all the people going back for seconds." He pointed his thumb over toward the table and took another scoop of his own.

"Well, how about that," she said. "They sure are."

Knowing that gave her great satisfaction.

Yes, Stanford is an idiot. Everyone has always said my dip is delicious. Except him.

"I wouldn't be surprised if everything you cook is good," Len said.

"My sister says I fix dishes just like mama did."

"Then there you go." Len nodded.

She beamed. Being with him made her heart happy. Even if he was older than she was, she liked him and was going to follow her heart.

"I'm really glad we met," she said.

"I'm glad too." He smiled back. "I'd like to learn more about you."

"What would you like to know?"

"What are your hobbies?"

"I love to go dancing, though it's been a while because I've been busy with school, job hunting and apartment hunting. I live with my sister, but I'm moving into a new place next week."

"Where are you moving?"

"I'll still be in Bartlett; I just can't keep living with my sister. It's time I was on my own, in my own apartment with no roommates."

"Just you and Mr. Whiskers?"

"That's right." She nodded. "I was in a sorority house in Kentucky, but then after my stalker, I moved in with Betsy and transferred to the University of Memphis. I didn't want to live away from family after what happened."

"I can see that."

"But I'm over it." She shrugged. "Ready to move on."

"Sounds like you're well on your way."

"I don't start at the Bartlett branch for another week and I'm in bank training at the main branch first," she said. "I might catch a matinee next week. Would you like to go?"

Thank you for taking the time to read *Check Out.*

If you enjoyed the story, please consider telling your friends and/or posting a review. Word of mouth is an author's best friend and much appreciated. Thank you!

- Debra Parmley

BONUS CONTENT:

Check Out Book Trailer: https://youtu.be/Hgj4QWBI9wU

Debra Reading the First Chapter of Check Out:
https://youtu.be/6uZG3ggMSow

Check Out is also available in audiobook:
https://www.audible.com/pd/Check-Out-Audiobook/B01IWM4SC8

Join Debra's Newsletter sign up: https://landing.mailerlite.com/webforms/landing/w9s9h0

ACKNOWLEDGMENTS

My thanks and appreciation to the team which almost brought this story to publication: my former editor Tamara Hoffa (RIP), and my proofreader, Shannon Ellis. You were a good team to work with. It is a shame the publishing house closed.

Thank you to my cover artist for Belo Dia Publishing Inc., Sheri L. McGathy for the new cover.

Special thanks and appreciation to my fight scene choreographer, Robert Arrow, and my USMC advisor, Charles Welshans. The fight scenes are entirely thanks to you both.

Thank you to my librarian advisor and first beta reader, Jocie McKade.

Thanks to my husband, aka my patron of the arts for many years, and to my family for their love and support.

For you, my readers, thanks and infinite love and gratitude for your unwavering love and support of my work.

Fascinated by fairy tales and folktales, ever since she was young, Debra Parmley has always ended her stories with a happy ever after. Every story she writes turns into a romance. She started out writing gritty western historical romance and damsel in distress stories. Her first book, A Desperate Journey, was traditionally published in 2008, after competing in the American Title II contest. A hybrid author, she went on to write for five publishers before branching out with her own Indie press, Belo Dia Publishing Inc. Belo Dia is Portuguese for Beautiful Day.

Debra writes historical romance, contemporary romance, dystopian romance and romantic suspense. An Air Force veteran's wife, she writes military heroes in the present and in the future. Debra's work in the travel industry gave her the opportunity to visit many countries. Her luggage often carried home folk tales from the countries visited. Her travel experiences are scattered throughout her books. Her three favorite things are dark chocolate, visiting the beach and ocean, and hearing from her readers. Each card, letter and email is a treasured gift, like finding a perfect shell upon the beach. For more information about Debra and her books, please visit Debra's website:

http://www.debraparmley.com

Follow Debra on;

Book Bub:

https://www.bookbub.com/profile/debra-parmley

Newsletter sign up: http://eepurl.com/ZUyC1

Goodreads: https://www.goodreads.com/DebraParmley

FB fan page:

https://www.facebook.com/authordebraparmley/

FB fan group:

https://www.facebook.com/groups/debraparmley/

FB page:

https://www.facebook.com/debra.parmley.7

Pinterest: https://www.pinterest.com/debraparmley/

Instagram: https://www.instagram.com/debraparmley/

To Catch An Elf (2020 release)

Through the Dunes (2020 release)

Dystopian Romance/SEAL hero:

The Hunger Roads Trilogy:

A Change of Scenery: Book One

Down a Back Road: Book Two (2020 release)

Into the Convergence Zone: Book Three (2020 release)

Holiday Romance:

Jenna's Christmas Wish

The Twelve Stitches of Christmas (co-author Robert Arrow)

A Three C's Ranch Christmas Wedding

To Catch An Elf (2020 release)

Medieval Fairy Tale Romance:

The Twelve Stitches of Christmas (co-author Robert Arrow)

Vague Directions (2020 release)

Historical Romance:

Western:

A Desperate Journey

Dangerous Ties

Deadly Adversaries

Desperate, Dangerous and Deadly: A Western Collection

American Mail Order Bride series:

Isabella: Bride of Ohio (co-author Robert Arrow) #17

1920's Butterflies Fly Free Series:

Trapping the Butterfly: Book One

Dancing Butterfly: Book Two

Exotic Butterfly: Book Three (2020 release)

Anthologies/Short Story:

Hansel and Gretel Anthology/The Sweetest Day

Wounded Heroes Anthology/Two Step, New Steps

We Know the Truth, Do You? /The Road to Groom Lake

More Monsters From Memphis/Vampire From Memphis

Poetry:

Twilight Dips – poetry anthology